APOGEE

A MAC SISCO NOVEL

APOGEE
A MAC SISCO NOVEL

BY

LOU EARLE

PHiR Publishing
San Antonio

PHiR Publishing
San Antonio, TX
phirpublishing.com

ISBN: 979-8-9867452-0-6
Library of Congress Control Number: 2022915209

Printed in the United States of America

Dedicated to my wife, Lynne, and daughter, Janie

for their unbridled encouragement and support

PROLOGUE

Something was wrong in America. Very wrong. As the ISIS/ISIL rampage was becoming a distant memory, tensions across the globe were elevating in other ways. The Middle East appeared to be the only constant—The Palestinians were still lobbing rockets across to the Israelis. Iranian-funded and trained factions were causing trouble here and there. But elsewhere, subtle changes were afoot, much like a tremor that precedes a major earthquake.

Historic international alliances were shifting. The EU was crumbling, and NATO was in conflict. The UK toiled with Brexit, while Eastern Europe withdrew to protect its historic borders. Tensions between Russia and Ukraine were at an all-time high. From Japan to the U.S., ever-increasing numbers of immigrants strained borders and relations in search of refuge from the violence and unrest of their homelands. Under the scourge of communism, formerly rich lands had lost their wealth and freedoms were crushed by corrupt leaders and false promises. Was this signaling a return of those dark days? Or was it business as usual? History is rife with examples of revolution and conflict between the government and the governed; but this was different. It wasn't here or there; it seemed to be everywhere. Societies were slowly breaking down, like a body succumbing to an indiscernible, progressive disease.

And while America was booming economically, new social ideologies were erupting that promised utopia while threatening the very pillars of its culture. The very bedrock of everything that was right about America was under attack, from several directions simultaneously. One of those phenomena, 'cancel culture,' was steamrolling its way across America. What most couldn't perceive, though, is that this was just a symptom of a much larger, endemic disease. One that we may have all been very carefully and purposefully infected with many, many years ago...

CHAPTER ONE

THE AGENCY

The large glass door closed silently behind him as the man strode confidently out into the brisk morning air. His final briefing had been grueling, and his new status had come as a surprise. After over ten years with the Agency and the last three in the 'building,' Mac Sisco had assumed his new assignment would be more of the same. Everything had been routine that day until his boss, the Super grade GS sixteen running G Group announced that their scheduled meeting had been preempted by a personal session on the top floor with the Director of the NSA.

On the surface, such an invitation was not overly remarkable. He knew Admiral James Clausen well enough and liked him, but his frequent field assignments had kept their interactions limited. Even as America was facing significant internal challenges, the grizzly four-star admiral had his hands full with the Chinese, North Koreans, and the Iranians, so this sudden face-to face felt strangely incongruous.

Clausen closed the dark, paneled doors of the secure office with a hiss. They were alone. "Good to see you again Mac, please take a seat," he said, gesturing to a chair next to the hand-carved walnut coffee table between them. The Admiral's tone was foreboding as he continued. "Let me get right to it—here's the sitrep. Since the election of our current President a year ago, he and the NSC have instructed this

Agency to go long on any and all threats to the governance of our country. We have been successful for some time now penetrating and exploiting all forms of digital communication from foreign threats worldwide, no matter what cyphers, codes, or encryption are used. Eventually, we break them all. We are highly proficient at undetected infiltrations into enemy organizations using carefully curated methods, irreproachable sources, and of course you and our special operations teams. This initiative is highly compartmented, even within the NSA, due to the extraordinary sensitivity. No other U.S. agency has been engaged or even read in."

He refilled his coffee, then continued. "There are strong indications certain elements of society are behaving in parallel to undermine the very foundations of our nation and its values, and the White House believes this cannot be a coincidence. In other words, we have real concerns there is a concerted effort underway to overthrow America. I know how this sounds, but if there is even the remotest chance this is actually happening, we must know, and act quickly. And I need your help."

Mac was stunned. Attempting to grasp the enormity of the Admiral's words, he asked, "Director, why me? This doesn't feel like it's in my wheelhouse."

"Fair question, Mac. I know you don't have experience with this type of thing. However, you *have* spent the last three years on complex intelligence assignments, all of which you successfully resolved. More importantly, all those cases required a very nuanced response. You navigated a web of very intricate criminal structures, established trust under deep cover, gleaned the essential intelligence, and used force appropriately to neutralize dangerous threats. It is fortuitous, actually, that your skillset has become honed to a sharp point at a time when it is most needed."

Mac had to agree the Admiral had him pegged. Mac was multilingual, fluent in five languages. His father had worked for the State Department, dragging Mac and his mother from country to country for nearly his entire childhood. And his decade of intelligence operations work had been anything but routine. As an ex-Navy Seal, he came to the Agency well prepared for a transition to field work. What followed was even more special operations training, additional survival school, and being read into several special CIA undercover programs that would prepare him for critical intelligence collection and analysis assignments. Overseas operations were a rarity for NSA officers, usually under the jurisdiction of the CIA. There were a few select specialists, however, that the Agency designated for these kinds of assignments and Mac had drawn the short straw.

At thirty-five and six feet one inches, his 180-pound frame was relatively unassuming. His passion for rock-climbing over the years had ingrained in him both a physical and mental toughness that to-date were continually underestimated. Fortunately, his rigorous Seal training followed by combat experience in Afghanistan formed the perfect foundation for six months of multi-intelligence agency Specops interdiction and survival skills programs.

It was true that Sisco's recent ops had been unique and especially challenging. In the last three years he brought two drug lords to justice, eliminated an international terrorist leader in Zimbabwe and debilitated the organization. Domestically, he eradicated the financial capabilities of a U.S.-based Marxist activist group that was stealing and selling intellectual property from universities and colleges across the nation.

The Admiral continued. "What makes this problem so tough is its scope. We're talking about assaults coming from several sectors within our country, and the intensity of it is severe. We all hear the daily rhetoric but tend to ignore it—we write them off as a few, overzealous crazies. Unfortunately, the scope and breadth of the activity and the speed of its evolution suggest there is something organized about it. That is what we need to understand. It has become clear that this movement is an existential threat to our country and our way of life.

"This program and all its underlying operations are classified Top-Secret SCI, code word FACET. When we can't meet face-to-face, you will report directly to me on this mission via a secure, grey phone line number." Then he paused, regarding Mac seriously. "America will never be destroyed from the outside. If we lose our freedoms, it will be because we have destroyed ourselves from within."

He's Paraphrasing Abraham Lincoln... This was a much bigger deal than Mac had foreseen. The list of infected elements left out few American institutions, with the American media right at the top. More insidious, however, was the U.S. educational system—from kindergarten all the way up through the entire university system. Global corporations and NGOs, the entertainment and sports industries, segments of local and state governments, and parts of the so-called 'swamp' of our federal government, including the judicial system. To make matters worse, there was evidence the disease had infected sections of the U.S. military and intelligence organizations.

Thankfully, the Admiral had a plan and Mac had been given carte blanche to execute it. While he was very comfortable working alone, he knew he would need help. Clausen had been very clear about that and identified several qualified candidates for his team. Mac was humbled by his confidence in him, but painfully aware the mission required expertise that no one person could possess; there was just too much territory to cover with too little time. They were going to have to call in some chits, maybe even do a little begging. The sun was just beginning its downward slide in a cloudless sky as the Admiral's limo rolled up beside a spotless silver Learjet, engines already running on the tarmac at Andrews for the trip south. Next stop, Austin, Texas.

CHAPTER TWO

AGAVE RANCH

Mac had reasons to set up shop in Texas. His parents owned a ranch in Wimberley, a quaint tourist destination in the hill country. He enjoyed visiting them; however, one real advantage was that his father had been the Ambassador to Israel and was a retired CIA intelligence officer as well. His counsel would be invaluable in deconstructing the complexities of this threat. The Admiral had already agreed to read him in.

Mac weaved through towering live oaks along the three-mile, crushed granite drive. Several horses, a herd of mini-Hereford cows and several barking dogs greeted him as he made the final turn into the Agave Ranch compound. Joseph Sisco and his wife, Winnie, greeted their son warmly as he met them halfway along the stone steps leading up to the house.

"Good to see you, Mac. How is the Pit?" His father chortled, referring to the bubble that was Washington, D.C.

"The longer I'm there, the more I understand how accurate that description is," Mac responded with a grin.

After a casual Texas barbecue dinner expertly prepared by Joe and Winnie, father and son relaxed together on the large porch overlooking the expansive pastures falling away to the south.

"I spoke with Jim Clausen after he met with you earlier today," Joe began. "Glad my Top-Secret clearance stays with me in retirement. My background investigation from my last job is still current. That said, some days it seems like a curse. Anyways, he said this was his idea and that you agreed. I'll help you in any way I can, but after hearing some of the details, it sounds like you're gonna need some serious help."

Mac nodded, taking a sip of sweet tea. "Yeah, the Admiral and I spent a lot of our time on that. The team must be small so we can respond instantly and remain flexible, but with a diversity of skillsets and depth of expertise sufficient to handle whatever we must flex to. So, each member must be responsible for several different disciplines. It's a tall order. But before I can build the team, what I need is help with understanding the threat. I mean, right now all I have is a lot of theory, and we're thin on facts. We don't have a definitive money trail, and we don't know who we're dealing with. You could make the argument that this whole thing is just a natural evolution of a broken, global society."

Ambassador Sisco leaned back in his chair and gazed out at the moonlit sky, then across the darkened fields dotted with cow silhouettes. "Well Mac, I hope you're wrong, because I can't even begin to imagine how to tackle the natural evolution of society," he said with a smirk. "But if this whole thing has in fact been engineered, and your admiral says the evidence for it is in all the files we need to review, then maybe there's a chance to reverse engineer it."

"Well dad, if there's anyone who can reverse-engineer something, it's probably you," Mac interjected.

"Well, not by myself, for sure," Joe replied. "You know, this whole thing seems so complicated that on the surface, it appears complex. We can't confuse the two. I think that's the tack we must take here—just because a problem has a lot of moving pieces doesn't mean it can't be understood. If we can identify enough touchpoints, document a comprehensive process flow that proves there is correlative decision making and specific intent, then we can assume it's man-made. Then we can try to discriminate between what is correlation and what is truly causal, and *those* associations will illuminate who the actors are—who and where the threat is. You must admit, it is extraordinary that so many factors have converged so conveniently across so many cultures. And they are all, in one way or another, leading society down the same path."

Their conversation turned to less important things, then to silence—both men engrossed in their own thoughts, interrupted only by the subtle night sounds of the starlit expanse before them. *The calm before the storm*, Mac thought.

CHAPTER THREE

RUBIK'S CUBE

It felt to Mac that as soon as his head hit the pillow, the glare of the larger-than-life Texas sun broke through the bedroom window and cut short his deep, but troubled sleep. Last night's conversation had stimulated a REM-filled night punctuated by broken images and fading memories of a dark, sweeping chaos.

After a hearty breakfast of eggs over easy, cured Canadian bacon, steaming yellow Texas grits and a brimming cup of black home ground Brazilian coffee, Mac and Joe moved into a large, wood-paneled study adjacent to the great room.

Joe opened the conversation. "First things, first. Before we dive into the details, I think we need to scope out the problem in general terms and then start to fill in the blanks. Once we have a basic understanding of that, we can begin to map out the process flow. That will also help us figure out what resources and skill sets you need on the team. Does that make sense?"

"Yes," Mac agreed. "But I don't want to get too far into it before engaging the team—they are likely to see things from different angles that we may not consider."

"Sure, let's compare notes," continued Joe. "So, I spoke with your boss, but even though it was a secure line, he kept it short. You have more information than I do, so you can start."

Mac pulled a pile of Top-Secret documents from his portfolio and set them in a tall stack between them. "According to Admiral Clausen and his staff, they have been collecting intel on this case for over a year, but it wasn't until about sixty days ago when they began to see a pattern forming. It was then that they launched a formal case under the Top-Secret Code word FACET. It's a FVEY mission, and they named it *Apogee*."

"Huh," the Ambassador said disapprovingly. "Even though the scope of this is global, I'm surprised it's being released to Five Eyes. The wider we go with this, the easier it will be for the enemy to find out we are onto them. Especially if this is as cabalistic as it sounds. And even with Five Eyes support, the mission is going to be incredibly difficult. There's just so much territory to cover." Five Eyes was a longstanding, critical intelligence partnership between Australia, Canada, New Zealand, the United Kingdom, and the United States. These five countries were also parties to the multilateral UKUSA Agreement, a treaty for joint cooperation in signals intelligence.

He continued. "The level of secrecy required just doesn't allow for many players. The risk of leaks is too great, and the consequences would be catastrophic. But I get it—this isn't a single problem, it's several problems. They are all interrelated, and we need to look to our allies for resources. We may come to a point where we think we've figured out one problem only to find it's an illusion, that we've made assumptions we shouldn't have made. Then we'll have to backtrack."

"Yeah, one false move could drive the bad guys underground," said Mac. "And can you imagine the panic if it went public? Figuring this out is going to take time. It's so complicated, there are so many different sides to it. Honestly, it should be codenamed *FACETS*, not *FACET*. Or even better, *Rubik's Cube*."

As the orange-red orb of an impossibly large Texas sun slowly disappeared over the horizon, the two men finally called it a day. The NSA's preliminary findings were strewn all over the room. Documents and brainstorming notes were taped to every wall. Lines of colored twine tacked at each end showed associations between elements. Rudimentary timelines showing temporal sequences and highlighting likely and possible causal relationships.

With a sigh, Mac leaned back to get a better view of the day's handiwork. "Well Dad, what have we got?"

Joe stood in the center of the room, arms folded across his chest. "There is no question in my mind that there are definitive patterns emerging. It isn't just the parallel activities and timelines; there are definitely non-societal drivers at play. Also, there is evidence of coordination between some of those activities and it's occurring at multiple levels. That points to a conspiracy."

"I agree," Mac said. "The other inescapable thing is the level of resources needed to foment and sustain all these disruptions. At the micro level you don't really notice it, but at the macro-level, it's hard to ignore. It's concerning that the timelines seem to be both synchronized and accelerating, almost as if there is a countdown, and we're nearing the end of something."

Mac's mind was racing. The possibilities were outrageous and the implications staggering. He had to get a handle on the problem fast.

He needed his team. Even as he drifted into a fitful sleep, he was filling in the blanks. Tomorrow would be a big day and he had to get on the road.

They were up early the next morning. The sky was darkening with a promise of rain. "I sure hope this isn't a bad omen," Mac commented, almost under his breath.

"I doubt it's related," laughed Joe. "Unlike the weather, we may be able to control the outcome. At the least, we should be able to do better than the weatherman, the forecast was for sunny skies."

"Dad, I put together a short list of who I think should be on the team. We can review that this morning and then I'm going to head out. I'd like to onboard everyone as soon as possible."

"I was thinking the same thing, Mac," his father answered. "Glad we're on the same page. Let's get to it."

The darkening skies kept their promise. Moving north at thirty-five miles per hour, however, the storm dropped two inches of rain and blew through in a couple hours, leaving a spectacular rainbow in its place. The change in weather was a welcome sight as Mac packed the rental car for his departure. He made a mental note that his analogy had been off; this wasn't a Rubik's Cube—it was far, far more complicated than that. The good news was, he and his father had agreed on the makeup of the team, a group well-equipped to help them begin to figure it out. The bad news—they were scattered all over the globe.

CHAPTER FOUR

TEAM BUILDING

Joe Franklin had just returned from a five-mile run in the hills off Route 285 just north of his San Antonio home and was about to hit the weights in his home gym when the doorbell rang. Forty years old now, Franklin was a retired commander and ex-Seal instructor. He was doing his best not to lose his edge. So far, it seemed to be working. The big man opened his front door with a yank, revealing the smiling face of his former student.

"Well, I'll be damned," he blurted out. "Mac Sisco, as I live and breathe."

"Good to see you, Joe! Looks like I interrupted your sweat bath."

"Don't worry about it buddy, it's time to finish up anyway. How about a beer?" Joe snagged two Buds from the fridge and smoothly tossed one to Mac. The two old friends walked through the living room to a patio off the back of the house. The modestly manicured back yard was bordered by a high wrought iron fence, nearly invisible behind a maze of purple and red Crepe Myrtles. Several mature trees and mulched beds dotted the smooth contours of the rich green zoysia lawn. An idyllic landscape.

"Wow Joe, you must either spend a lot of money or a lot of time out here."

Franklin laughed. "Both, actually. It's how I de-stress from the trials of retirement."

"Trials?" Mac quipped.

"Sure. It's pretty simple. When we worked together in the field, it was intense, dangerous. An absolute rush. Then, retirement. It's like being in a Nascar race, and then your engine blows. Two hundred to zero in an instant. I've tried rock-climbing, triathlons, halo ski diving. A dozen other crazy stunts. But there's nothing out there that compares. It's only been a year, and I am already flat out bored! I'm glad you stopped by—we can at least reminisce about it a little bit."

Sisco couldn't help smiling to himself at his old friend's frustrations. He wasn't sure that Franklin would be available, let alone amenable. They tipped back their beers in unison. "As it turns out, this is not just a friendly visit. I have an agenda, one that could satisfy that nasty itch you're feeling."

The big Veteran tipped his beer back again, taking a long draught. He leaned forward, eyes narrowing as he crumpled the can with one hand. "Let's hear it."

"OK, I'll start with the abridged version." Mac went on to give him a summary of the mission.

When he was done, Franklin gave him a perplexed look. "Seriously? I've seen this show, and it's called *The Blacklist*. Are you fucking with me?"

"Well, there's a whole range of societal movements that were well camouflaged in the beginning but are now becoming common and other pieces seemed to be linked together artificially. For example, many new quasi-insurgent groups with different names seem to be popping up. And they're not just copycats trying to get funding. They are cooperating and synchronizing their disruptions. We are also seeing coordination between disparate non-governmental social structures like academia, the mainstream media and vocational groups adopting consistent positions and campaigns."

"Ok, Mac, so what you are saying is that there is a global conspiracy with shadowy figures pulling strings all over the planet, right? I hate to state the obvious, but there's no way something this big could be kept a secret."

"I know it sounds far-fetched," Mac replied, "but NSA Sigint supports this theory and Admiral Clausen agrees. And it's more like the shadowy figures are setting things in motion, then nurturing and redirecting when needed. These groups don't even realize that they are part of it."

Franklin watched him speculatively, then continued. "Well, assuming this is legit, what is the play and why are you telling me all this?"

"Joe, Clausen has committed NSA resources to this, but he's got to keep it tightly compartmented. We need a human intelligence team on the ground. Because the potential for compromise is so high, we must keep this small and tight knit. We are going to utilize some highly specialized talent from Five Eyes, but we are not even sharing this gig with any of the other U.S. intelligence organizations. That might come full circle and bite us in the ass at some point. Bottom line, I am putting the team together. You are my first choice, so are you ready to rumble?"

His face erupted in an enormous grin. "You had me at *satisfy that nasty itch*. So, when do we start?"

Mac's comeback was immediate. "Right now."

CHAPTER FIVE

THE ENEMY WITHIN

Twenty-seven hundred miles north and fifteen miles west of Philadelphia, Pennsylvania, the city of brotherly love, a very different conversation was taking place. Flanked by suburbs and traversing many smaller towns along the way, its namesake railroad meandered all the way to Columbia. The electric Paoli Local was another downtown commuting alternative to the Schuylkill (affectionately dubbed the *Surekill*) expressway. Bryn Mawr was an affluent area just a few stops from city center. Impeccably manicured grounds surrounded the numerous mansions gracing its heavily treed bluffs. One of the grandest properties sat high on a hill, protected by a massive, gated rock entrance. The perimeter treatment of the ten-acre lot was as impressive as the entrance, with four-meter-high iron fencing blanketed by dense hedging from top to bottom.

The original homestead had been constructed over 100 years before with imported granite and hardwoods in oversized dimensions. Four stories of sprawling edifice that had been tastefully expanded over the years as the needs of its owners and their pocketbooks grew. Today, it encompassed thirty thousand square feet. As eye opening as the exterior was, the interior upped the ante.

Wandering hallways of stone terminated in conforming ten-foot, solid walnut doors. Three wings with seven guest suites radiated out from the main structure. Each had its own bath, fireplace, and sitting area, and each sported a balcony overlooking the exquisite gardens and pools interconnected by immaculate, crushed red granite pathways.

The main level opened into several functional areas with granite walls climbing seven meters to ornate paneled ceilings and hand painted mid-eighteenth-century scenes. Each room was fronted by large stone arches framed by polished cherry doors adorned with brass fixtures. The primary living room's mammoth walk-in stone fireplace was a sight to behold, with its hand-hewed mesquite wood mantel. Leather and cowhide furnishings added a subtle southwest allure to otherwise very European surroundings.

A door off the west wall led to a large, wood paneled study. Next to it, a music room with an ebony Steinway grand piano at one end and at the other, an antique organ with pipes built right into the ornate ceiling. The dining room floor had been lowered four feet to accommodate an enormous, intricately carved twenty-foot-high breakfront imported in two pieces from Africa over a half century ago. A massive companion dining table with matching chairs stretched the length of the room, promising gluttonous adventures for up to thirty guests. A breathtaking, curved open stairway to the second story invited even more exploration.

Next to the dining room, Peter Gunderson stood straight-backed in the center of his opulent library. He was an imposing figure for a sixty-six-year-old, weighing in at a hardened 195 pounds and all of six feet three inches. He made daily use of the well-equipped gym and the seven miles of trails. Gunderson had lived here his whole life. His grandfather built the house in the late 1800's after emigrating from Germany. His skills as an investment banker had ensured a steady and growing income, made more rewarding by a lack of taxation during that era. Gunderson's father took the fortune to even greater heights when he made all the right bets during the great depression and the subsequent needs of a world at war in the 1940's.

He was among the wealthiest on the planet. *It's a good thing,* he would often think, because he was committed to a very expensive and time-consuming project where vast resources were just one of the prerequisites for participation. Urgent voices and echoing footsteps fast approaching broke him from his reverie.

"We must do something now, before things get out of hand."

"Calm down Nicholi, we need more information first. Once we are sure about the facts, we can decide how to triage."

Gunderson turned to face the two men, now patiently silent and side-by-side before him. His stern demeanor was unnerving to most, and frustratingly unreadable to all. After an interminable moment of silence, he spoke. His words were soft with a threatening undertone. "I trust your outbreak is worthy of my attention?"

Jefferey Gunderson, Peter's only child, knew better than to play games. He didn't realize his father was in the house and had let his guard down. His debate with Krishinko was sloppy, and his father heard him. "My apologies dad, we thought you were outside. We'll get back to you when we've resolved the issue and have appropriate recommendations."

Nicholi Krishinko, Gunderson's Slavic commissar, interjected. "Sir, Jeff and I will certainly come up with contingencies, but I believe the urgency of the situation warrants an immediate response, and I think we could use some counsel."

Gunderson did not like impromptu or premature brainstorming. There was too much at stake. Their strategy, codenamed *Genplan*, was particularly vulnerable in these final stages. After decades of camouflaged, incremental manipulations, the pieces were finally coming together and soon his life's work (and that of three generations of his decedents) would finally be realized. Guided by the iron will of Gunderson's grandfather, his father's, and now his own, the family legacy was close to coming to fruition.

The genesis of their ideology was simple enough: strong discontent with the perpetual mediocrity of the masses and the unflappable belief that a small, powerful, elite ruling class was crucial to turning things around. His family's obsession with this vision endured and became stronger with each succeeding generation.

The Gunderson patriarchs had been patient, recognizing that worldwide control was not achievable within a single lifetime. They also understood the dynamics of social change on a macro scale. Everything they did was enabled by their vast fortune and leverage with a select, carefully curated group of world leaders. Their plan had been refined over time—targets defined and eliminated, surgical strikes and invasions even—all carefully planned and executed.

Knowing that whole generations needed to be converted, they began with the educational systems. While time consuming, this was among the easiest endeavors with the highest probability of success. The young are naive and easy to manipulate. Educators, particularly in higher education, have a false sense of superiority, one that was all too easy to feed and take advantage of. These vulnerabilities are consistent across societies and cultures, so implementation was vastly simplified.

The movers and shakers in the financial world are a more troublesome target. Early on, the Gundersons struggled and made little headway. The variations of and differences between governance and business structures were so pronounced that no intervention could effectively be sustained. Furthermore, periodic wars and the resultant power shifts did not allow them to make a foothold in global finance until the mid-1900s. After the Second World War ended, however, things began to settle down. With the invention of the computer, technology advances in travel, shipping and communications coupled with diminished nationalism spawned a whole new wave of worldwide commerce and globalization—the dynamic shrinking of distance on a large scale—was born. The resultant ubiquity of instant communication and financial transactions, ease of travel, and rapid improvement of standards of living worldwide leveled the playing field for everyone—a commonality that allowed societal control and manipulation to be manifested within corporations and governments in less obtrusive or obvious ways. Globalism was the penultimate gift that allowed their plan to move forward and begin to accelerate.

As industries began to thrive, enormous capital and resources became more accessible and controllable. It was Gunderson who had done the lion's share of work in this regard, and it was the most important element of the plan. His global investment background and reach positioned him to engage with government and industry leaders on every continent. His influence and access were unparalleled, and in the last decade he had materially influenced the directions of some of the world's most powerful organizations.

With this leverage, the final targets were surprisingly easy to topple. Mass media fell into line quickly as they followed the money. Celebrities in all quarters were herded like sheep, as if by an invisible but unrelenting force. Because victimization of the people was the primal message, the monied crowd could not resist virtue signaling or the urge to use their podiums to move the whole thing along. Politicians pandered for votes as politicians do, but money and media won the day. All that was left was the people. As planned, his strategy was now self-propelled and had passed a point of no return. Success was nearly inevitable.

Before its final realization, however, the 'people' part had to be completed, at least to a certain degree—there had to be a tipping point. Gunderson struggled mightily with defining this outcome. Organizations were controllable, individuals en mass—not so much. He knew he had them by the short hairs. They were between a rock and a hard place with government, media, and the judiciary on one side and regional and global business on the other. Furthermore, the younger generation, well-indoctrinated at this point, were pushing from underneath. Things were going well. But even so, Gunderson was worried about *boiling the frog*.

Jeffery Gunderson had followed in his father's footsteps, attending Haverford College, a small, elite school. After graduating with honors, he continued his education at the University of Pennsylvania, then launched his career in a New York based firm practicing international law. After five years, his father wooed him back to Philadelphia to be his Senior Vice President of Global Operations and Legal Counsel. It was not a serendipitous appointment. Gunderson had been grooming his son for years to take his rightful place by his side.

Six months ago, Gunderson called Jefferey into his private study and shared his concern. After a long day of Zoom meetings with operators in Asia and the Middle East, Jefferey was just about to leave their basement offices under the main house.

"Son, would you mind staying for a drink? I have something important to discuss." It was a cold and dreary day as the two sat across from each other, each brandishing a twenty-year-old single malt scotch in front of a roaring fire in the massive stone fireplace. "I've been thinking a lot about the final stage of our efforts, and I have a concern."

The young Gunderson waited patiently as the pause he was all too familiar with settled over them.

Then, his father continued. "There is a theory called the boiling frog concept which may come into play in the final phase. We haven't yet had to deal with it because our work has always been focused on organizational behavior, and this is about individual behavior." After another pause and a healthy hit from his glass, he continued. "How do you keep a live frog from jumping out of a pot of boiling water?"

His son looked at him quizzically.

Gunderson continued. "In order to cook the frog, you must turn up the heat and boil the water, but when the water gets too hot, the frog jumps out because it feels pain. But if you turn up the heat gradually...the frog is slowly conditioned to the increasing temperature and doesn't realize he is being cooked. He will just sit there and eventually die."

Jefferey's quizzical look morphed to a tentative grin. "Why not just put a lid on the pot?"

"Because we have too many pots and not enough lids. You don't want one frog without a lid to see or hear what is happening to the frog next door. Here's the bottom line. I need you to stop what you are doing and to focus on this. Put a team together with our top Commissars come up with an executable plan to make sure that the masses, the people, stay conditioned."

"How far do you want me to go?" Jefferey asked.

"If the people begin to realize what is going on—if they organize and rise up, it would be an existential threat to the entire Genplan," his father replied. "Everything is at stake. Don't spare the rod. If anyone gets in your way, take them out."

CHAPTER SIX

REUNION

Mac was out in Fredericksburg at Enchanted Rock Park on his third solo pitch and knew he was in trouble. It was a five four climb, but he was rusty. His hand jam slipped, and he was falling. He had only a couple seconds to fall as the ground raced up at him. Then he woke up, sweat covering his face and soaked into his bedsheets. *That was too real,* he thought.

Franklin was already up and about. After three days of grinding through videoconferences, this was their last day at his place. "Sleeping in cowboy?" He greeted Mac with a wide grin. "You look worse than I feel."

"I revisited some of my old climbs and it did not go well," Mac groaned. "I hope it's not a harbinger for the days ahead."

"Nothing a good cup of java and some grits and eggs can't cure," Franklin smiled, as he filled Mac's plate to the brim.

The sleek private jet cut through the sky at thirty-five thousand feet, clouds hanging like desert dunes below under glaring sunshine that shot across the horizon. Mac and Franklin were three hours into their flight and beginning a descent into La Guardia. But their destination wasn't the Big Apple. They were headed to an out of the way beach house in Stone Harbor, New Jersey, a popular upscale favorite for New York and Philadelphia weekend warriors. It was a well-disguised safehouse purchased by the NSA almost twenty years before, from the estate of a deceased real estate mogul who died just as his mansion was completed.

On the lower half of the island, it was perched on a gentle rise in the middle of a long stretch of imported sand beachfront. The house was built to withstand everything an angry Atlantic Ocean could throw at it. A high, reinforced concrete foundation anchored the 10,000 square foot Tuscan mansion. Shatterproof windows protected by 200 mph-rated shutters ensured the all-rock structure would shrug off anything, from an historic storm surge to a hurricane. The perimeter was protected by a concrete wall that ran discretely along the beachfront. State of the art communications and servers were housed in an adjacent facility connected to the main house by a covered walkway.

While the residence was impressive, it didn't necessarily stand out from the neighboring estates. This end of the island was last to be built up in a cascade of newer real estate development on the island. During an unusual lull in the market, large tracts were snapped up by deep-pocketed urbanites looking for posh retreats only a couple hours away (minutes by helicopter) from both New York and Philadelphia. Hidden in plain sight, the property served perfectly as an NSA black site operations hub and secretive meeting place. Its cover was real enough. Legal and other documentation showed the home was owned by an eccentric multi-millionaire whose global travel allowed only short visits to each of his ten homes across the world. When he was there, he often entertained and held international meetings and conferences.

When travelling, his business partners, colleagues and friends were allowed access. Consequently, the neighbors would find nothing unusual about the roar of a Sikorsky's blades as it settled in, almost gracefully, on the helipad.

"Just like old times," Franklin yelled as he trotted hunkered down beneath the wash of the massive rotors.

"As they say, Joe, getting there is half the fun. I hope you enjoyed the ride because the other half may be a long time in coming," Mac yelled back. "It will be good to see some of the old crew. Carrie should already be here."

"I'll bet she got here hours ago just so she could slobber over all the tech in the ops center and still have time to head to the beach before the sun goes down," quipped the big Seal.

"I think she went straight to the beach, and I could use some fresh air, so I'll check there. You can look in the ops center. If she's not there, come find me." Mac responded.

At 34 years old, Carrie Swan was among the world's most accomplished computer technologists. While her primary discipline was AI, she was also experienced with advanced software development and hardware chip design. She graduated from Stanford, then followed with a doctorate from MIT in Artificial Intelligence Systems. As if that wasn't enough, she enrolled in Princeton to complete a second PhD in Advanced Computing Integration, a cutting-edge field focused on innovation in technology miniaturization and software self-awareness. Every U.S. intelligence agency had their eyes on her. But Swan valued her freedom and wanted control over how she lived her life. She rejected every offer. The Director, Homeland Security won her over by appealing to her sense of patriotism and convinced her to operate as a special independent contractor for all U.S. Intelligence Agencies. Since then, she had participated in field ops for each of them many times and was seldom without an assignment.

While a super-nerd at heart, Swan was also a fitness nut. No sport was too challenging, and competition was her fuel. Having grown up on the California coast, surfing was inevitable, but catching the Big One wasn't enough for her. She competed regularly in her home state and Hawaii, and even won a few amateur competitions. She stood out in a crowd. Five feet ten and a sinewy 135 pounds, straight blond locks, and narrow hips. A regimen of running, weight training and daily Crav Maga made her a true fitness specimen belied by her slender frame and somewhat hidden by her typically loose clothing. But Swan's most alluring quality was her intelligent, piercing, green eyes. She could capture anyone's attention immediately—it was difficult to look away.

Mac had teamed up with her a half dozen times over the past few years. On one occasion, while under heavy terrorist fire, she deactivated a bomb in a hotel and saved hundreds of lives, including Mac's. She was the real deal, and he knew he could count on her.

Mac trudged across a sand dune fronting the beach. It was late afternoon. Five or six people walked along the ocean's edge, heads down, searching for a conch or unique piece of driftwood to adorn their mantle or coffee table. A treasure hunter with large headphones and a Boston Red Sox baseball ball cap held a digger grate in one hand as he waved a high-end metal detector with the other. About a hundred yards out on the water, he saw a figure churning against the current through the roiling waves. Carrie. Who else would brave the infamous riptide on this part of the island long after the lifeguards had left for the day?

She emerged glistening ten minutes later, her hair matted and salty water dripping to the powdery sand. Her green eyes locked on Mac and she recognized him, her stride quickening slightly. She walked up with arms extended and gave him a cordial hug. "Mac, it's great to see you. It has been too long."

"You too, Carrie. What's it been, maybe a year?"

"At least."

"I'm glad you agreed to jump in on this with me," Mac said. "As you may suspect, this one is, well, different."

"Yeah, no kidding. In any case, it's been a few weeks since I've had an op and once I heard your pitch... Let's just say I'm intrigued and looking forward to it."

As they arrived back at the compound, Mac noticed a black Mercedes S Class sedan parked out front. More of the gang arriving, Pat Curry and Peter Singe. Their final member, Elaine Warsaw, was delayed at a conference in London. She was the final day's keynote. Once off the stage, she would be whisked away to a private hangar at Heathrow to board a plain white Gulf Stream G250 bound for New York.

To say the team was eclectic would be an understatement. Clausen gave Mac an Agency wish list but vetting and selection was left to Mac. He and his father had poured over the list of candidates, reviewing their skills, knowledge, personality, and experience (and gut perception) against various possible threat scenarios to whittle down the list. Mac felt good about the choices they'd made. Now, the question was, could they convince the fantastic four to come on board. They would spend most of the next day on that task.

Each member was, or was close to being tops in their areas of specialty on a global scale. Aside from that, they all possessed several crucial common attributes—prerequisites for being on Clausen's list. They were all fiercely patriotic. They cherished independence, were all accountable, their integrity was unwavering, and they worked harder and smarter than everyone else. Finally, they had all been wooed into intelligence service years before from varied backgrounds and had been extensively trained in counter terrorism, special operations, and undercover assignments. They were smart, tough, and dedicated to the mission and the team. Both Mac and Franklin had worked with each of them at one point or another, under fire or otherwise, and they'd always come out the other side.

Peter Singe was a little fried after fifteen hours in the air. He was intimately familiar with the flight from Tokyo to LA, it was always a killer. Fortunately, the layover for his connection to New York was tight, and re-connecting with Pat Curry on the last leg was a pleasant experience for the two friends. Each in their late thirties, they were old school buddies and had known each other for years. As their 767 winged its way east, they chatted about old times and their recent adventures, carefully avoiding any reference to their current project. The flight was a nail biter, with turbulence slamming the plane around like a rowboat in the North Atlantic. The cabin went ominously quiet, as they tend to do in these situations. But the two old friends were oblivious to it. This was a cakewalk compared to a forty-year-old C-130 transatlantic jaunt, or a HALO jump out over the Amazon.

Singe's father founded an engineering consulting firm in the sixties, at a time when Japan was well into rebuilding its commercial power. The Japanese saw the wisdom in Malcolm Baldridge's innovative quality process management and demand for experts to navigate the transformation of their industries was high. The company prospered, and with it the family's fortunes. Consequently, Singe's desire to study abroad became a reality.

After graduating from the University of Tokyo with a BS in electrical engineering (and following in his father's footsteps), Singe moved to the United States and enrolled at the University of Chicago where he earned a masters in aeronautical engineering. His keen interest in all things with wings motivated him to acquire his pilot's license and eventually, a multiengine rating.

Small in frame but wiry and fit, he was naturally athletic. When he wasn't flying, he was sailing on Lake Michigan. From Catamarans to full-keel racing sloops, Singe loved this interaction with nature and the solitary rush of it all.

Pat Curry was an Aussie in every way. He was a brawny six feet four and 215 pounds with wavy light brown hair that just wouldn't hold a part. An intimidating figure with chiseled features and piercing eyes. His physical strength came not from working out or lifting weights, but from sport. He was a four-year starter for his high school rugby team and later competed as an adult. He played so well he once received an invitation to a pro team tryout, which he promptly turned down as it sounded too much like work. With water and wind his constant companion in his hometown of Sydney, Curry turned to sailing as well and crewed on several Americas Cup class sloops. He also competed in the Australia Day Regatta several years in a row. No one could winch in a heavy jib in a hard tack under stiff winds or tame an unruly spinnaker on a downwind run faster than Pat Curry.

While unsettling, his rough demeanor belied a gregarious personality that was as big as his physical size. And though Curry was something of a gentle giant, those who knew him well knew of his stern resolve and disciplined intellect. His father was a Colonel in the Australian military, cut down early in the Iraq war during a ferocious firefight while clearing a building sheltering enemy intelligence operations.

Curry's mother was a real estate broker. Whenever he wasn't in school, he'd help out. It soon became apparent that Curry had a knack for numbers and made short work of complex closings and contract negotiations. It was almost as if he knew intuitively what was needed to make everybody happy and to close the deal.

It was no surprise when Curry enrolled in the University of Sydney and majored in international finance, but no one predicted he would then choose to attend the University of Chicago Law School. That's where the two old friends first met. And the rest, as they say, is history.

The team met on the beachfront patio under a full moon. A row of tiki torches flickered at the edge of the white sands, throwing shadows outward toward the surf. Their dinner consisted of steamed clams, sweet corn, and Maine lobster, all laid out unapologetically. on the long table. Two buckets of craft beer and several bottles of wine completed the picture. Plates piled high with gourmet fare; each member of the team relished the rare, government-funded five-star treatment.

As anyone who has served in the military knows, sleep when and where you can because you never know when you'll get another chance. After eating and catching up, the soldiers on the team excused themselves and headed to their quarters. Mac was whipped. As he was leaving, Curry and Singe pulled him aside.

"Hey Mac, how real is all of this?" Curry asked, concerned. "I mean, I get it that maybe we haven't heard the whole story yet, and maybe it really is all organized at some high level. But even so, something so decentralized and self-powered... These things tend to just keep going, even after you take out the leadership. The Taliban, ISIL, al Qa'ida..."

Mac nodded. "Well Pat, that is—"

Before he could continue, Singe cut in. "I agree. I'm not sure if there's anything we can do to control the outcome."

Mac saw the genuine concern on their faces, and he understood it. *These guys are pros, and they were always all-in, no matter the odds. But they always knew the plan and had an exit strategy. They also knew that even the best plan can fail in multiple ways. Contingencies were critical.* "I hate to tell you guys, but I am not sure that I can tell you anything that will help you sleep better tonight. Our strategy is complex. For instance, one element of it requires at least a layman's understanding of thermodynamic theory. I don't think I can explain...that you will absorb and understand it all without good night's sleep. I don't even have all the details yet. I promise by this time tomorrow, we'll all have more to go on."

CHAPTER SEVEN

THE BUTTERFLY EFFECT

It was still dark when his cell buzzed the next morning. He knew who it was, and what was coming.

"Rise and shine Mac," Swan boomed. "Surfs up!"

"Come on Carrie, it's 6 am," Mac complained.

She laughed. "Get your butt moving and meet Joe and me on the patio for a run."

Mac groaned for affect. "Give me three minutes." He threw off the comforter, swung his legs to the floor, and grabbed his sneakers.

Elaine Warsaw arrived at 7. She knew the drill and despite a lack of sleep, she was ready to go. The consummate professional. An unflappable Brit with just enough OCD to believe there was a specific, correct place for everything, and that everything should be in its place. She had a PhD in Cultural Anthropology and another in Social Systems Dynamics, an emerging discipline focused on modern cultural and societal behaviors.

After Mac, Warsaw was the one other person that Clausen required to be on the team. Mac worked with her in Colombia to dismantle a multinational drug cartel that had infiltrated the government. It was a delicate assignment requiring a surgical approach. One wrong move could have precipitated an international incident and undermined regional security and stability. Warsaw spent six months analyzing the organization and became intimately familiar with the personalities, habits, daily activities and relationships of the drug lords, their lieutenants, and the compromised politicians. When she was ready, she orchestrated a strategy to create mistrust between them all, ultimately leading to their undoing. It was executed almost flawlessly, with minimal bloodshed. She and Mac worked tirelessly together in-country until they were pulled out, task complete. He greatly respected her intellect, competency, and attention to detail.

With auburn hair in a pageboy cut that neatly framed her delicate, angular features, she could best be described as professionally attractive. A dozen top-tier universities in as many countries offered her tenured professorships, but Warsaw valued her independence and opportunity for travel. She believed her best research would be achieved through multiple sources. Her solution was adjunct professorships at Oxford, Yale, Stanford and Cambridge, and research grants from several others.

Her associations with the Agency had been limited. While risky at times, she found it to be very rewarding work and this op was no different. The assignments were always exciting and the insights she gained were unique and valuable to her discipline.

Warsaw was a serious, but practical academic. She was a proficient and respected public speaker. For all her star power, however, she maintained a fun-loving attitude fueled by a very British, dry sense of humor. At 32, she was just getting started and enjoying every minute of the ride.

The run was exhilarating, the surf crashing and roiling as if urging them on as they clipped along the hard-packed sand. At a seven-minute mile pace, they were back to the patio in just over an hour, with plenty of time to wash up and meet with the rest of the team. The operations center building was a single-story structure with high ceilings resembling a high school gym. It boasted an Olympic indoor pool, weight room, locker rooms with saunas, a hot tub, showers, and a recreational area with a lounge, kitchen, and bar.

Invisible from outside scrutiny, the ops center was below ground and equally as large as the main floor. With its own series of functional rooms and facilities, it was accessed via a staircase behind a hidden door in the rec room. The entire lower level was sound and bomb proof. It was also protected against chemical, biological, and radiation attacks. There was a large conference room, several private offices, a kitchen and dining area, a walk-in weapons locker, a communications room, power systems backup and generator facility, and a computer and network center with state-of-the-art parallel processor-based servers, encryption systems and 5G+ networking. The antenna array for communications was an NSA-developed matrix built into the frame and roof of the building—completely undetectable. An underground garage housed four sedans and six motorcycles in the event a quick departure was called for. The exit ramp rose to the surface and was invisible beneath a sports court behind the building, surfaced with AstroTurf and capable of opening silently in less than ten seconds.

As Mac gazed at the team seated around the oversized ebony table, he couldn't help thinking, *the taxpayers would raise holy hell if they ever found out about this place...* "Great to see all of you again, despite the circumstances. You've all been briefed separately at a high level on the mission, and the operational framework and security protocols that have been put in place. Today, I will fill in the gaps and over the next five days, we will map out the details, assignments, and contingencies. Apogee liftoff will be at 0800 hours on day six. While we will stay engaged for as long as it takes, the mission timeline is tentatively planned for 30 days. Please hold your questions until I'm finished.

"Now, the first part of this overview is a bit sci-fi, so listen up and stay with me..."

Two hours later Mac switched off the big screen and looked into the dazed eyes of five of the brightest minds on the planet. "Any questions?" he asked. As he expected, the room erupted.

The NSA's longitudinal assessment was thorough and credible, but the methodology of the analysis equated to a paradigm shift for all of them. For instance, AI modeling was used to develop their overall strategy to mitigate and remove the threat. There were just too many weak connections—it was far too complex for the human mind to make complete sense of. The Agency's theory was based on several scientific concepts, concluding that a multitude of worldwide disruptive activities were linked, and that the conspiracy that was controlled by a single, cabalistic organization. They also surmised it had been going on for decades, in part because of the societal and cultural drivers involved. This was where the fun began. The assumption was derived from the thermodynamic Law of Entropy. Without efforts to the contrary, any state will evolve to a point of disorder over time. Disorder is a relative condition, which by definition necessitates a comparison, or ground state.

And there was the rub—a paradox. If the world was becoming more and more disrupted and unpredictable, it should be measurable entropy. A natural occurrence. *Not so fast* the analysts said. Civilization had been evolving over thousands of years in exactly the opposite direction, moving relentlessly to a more ordered existence. Why then, had it suddenly reversed directions? Even a fifty-year deterioration was an eye blink over thousands of years of human evolution. Thus, the conclusion suggested there must be a concerted force directed by someone or something to change that direction from order to disorder. Of course, the NSA only came to this conclusion after years of crunching mountains of data through their AI algorithm. Then the NSC briefed POTUS who directed the NSA to create a Top-Secret exploratory program to firm up their assessment and conceive multiple alternatives for targeting the threat. This led ultimately to the genesis of Apogee.

The world had serious problems, and many were generally aware but oblivious to what was causing them. The progression of it was insidious. Disruptions were infecting countries and cultures, and some *seemed* to have rather obvious global causes, but they were largely considered 'nationalistic' problems. It made no sense that a U.S. social problem would be replicated elsewhere, despite the great inertia of globalization. It was implausible that so many similar negative events would significantly impact entirely different and geographically separated cultures.

Deep in the bowels of NSA headquarters, frenetic activity was underway. A special series of offices were sectioned off. Blue seals were adorned on the doors, restricting all but a very narrow scope of Top-Secret SCI-cleared personnel from entry. The latest AI technology was transferred from their testing labs as soon as it was ready. The Agency's best were assigned to the core Apogee team, reporting directly to the Director.

Admiral Clausen cleared his calendar, delegated all but his most pressing duties and dug in. Analytics intel began to flow in, each report stamped with the ominous five letters that only a select few would recognize. FACET. With part of the team working on the root causes of disruption, money trails, and the identification of the those responsible, another group was busy deliberating how to stop it. The biggest challenge was overcoming the enormous inertia of it all.

The team understood that at this point, eliminating the conspirators would have little material effect on the well-established drivers that were pushing the world into chaos. It was postulated as well that the increasing frequency of such calamities might mean it was already past the point of no return. And finally, what was the end game? *Why* did they put this in motion? They needed to get inside the heads of their adversaries. What would the world look like, and how would it be governed if the team failed?

They organized into shifts, toiling relentlessly around the clock. They used powerful, advanced artificial intelligence systems to analyze all facets of the problem. NSA's basement housed the largest computer complex in the world with huge arrays of super servers capable of decrypting enormously complex code with nearly infinite permutations and combinations.

The NSA's AI servers were continuously self-learning, applying improved logic nanosecond by nanosecond. Even so, it still took weeks for their first models to generate some basic theorems. But once they had that in place, things accelerated rapidly. By the time Mac and his team had arrived at the compound in Stone Harbor, the final edits were being made to an operational approach that could be implemented in the field. The plan was based on scientific theory tangential to the thermodynamics of entropy. That close association made the analysts even more confident that they were on the right track.

Chaos theory had been around for years. Applying it to this kind of problem was, however, quite novel. The problem they were attempting to solve was fractal, nonlinear. Like the weather or stock market. Unpredictable. The idea was, if we can recognize and understand patterns of data within these super-complex ecosystems, we may be able to do something similar with socioeconomics and mitigate or avoid outcomes detrimental to our collective futures.

In the course of their analysis, an entirely different discovery offered them a fresh perspective. It was a butterfly effect concept, of sorts. And although the butterfly effect is essentially cause and effect with multiple degrees of separation, ostensibly something a computer could be programmed to figure out, it wasn't unearthed by their AI systems. It was a career NSA analyst, close to retirement, with a master's degree in physics from the University of Maryland who came up with it.

If a butterfly flapping its wings in South America could cause a tsunami off the coast of Japan, it should follow that the right actions, executed at exactly the right time, could reverse the damage. For the weary analysts in the building and the Director in the executive offices of the Agency, the idea of it was welcomed, offering a small window of hope for a positive outcome. If disruptive influences could be engineered and unleashed on society, they might be neutralized and reversed by opposing stimuli. In fact, because the current socioeconomic environment was so easily influenced, new stimuli could have an even greater impact.

After weeks of working on the 'butterfly effect' theory, the NSA team felt it was in fact a breakthrough, and it generated a kind of euphoria. Almost as if they had found a cure for cancer. Though untested, it increased their hope for a positive outcome.

The heavy lifting still needed to be done, however. How do we engineer the return to order and normalcy? It was time for their AI to really kick in. Compute heavy modeling was launched to determine the pressure points to undo the damage across societal elements. Individuals and organizations complicit in driving disruptions were identified and appropriate leverage and tactics were developed to reverse their direction and repair their damage. Once every conceivable target was identified with an offsetting remediation, they beta tested it to validate their work. Even with the massive servers churning twenty-four-seven, it took several days to complete the run. The results were not perfect, but the flaws were soon mitigated. They re-tested and the plan was refined. Satisfied that any more manipulation would be non-productive, they decided the plan was good to go.

There were risks everywhere, numerous opportunities for things to go sideways. But they'd worked hard and believed in the result, so they sent it upstairs. Clausen poured over it, spent a day cross-examining each analyst, then made calls to trusted sources for counsel. The next morning, he too sent it upstairs with his recommendations to launch Apogee. Two days passed as the National Security Council reviewed the material and vetted the sources. Clausen entertained numerous calls from aides and principles and at the end of the first day his sources confirmed that it was now with POTUS.

The next morning, the Admiral reviewed and organized the reports on his desk as they came in. Then the call came, sooner than he expected. He picked up the secure phone.

"Clausen."

His assistant was on the other end. "Director, the President is on the line."

"Thank you, Martin, please connect him."

"Good morning Jim, how are you holding up?"

"I'm doing fine, Mr. President. Thank you for asking. I trust your day is going well."

"It is, it is. It's a beautiful day. Listen, I won't keep you long. I've reviewed your work with the DNI, and we both think it is exemplary. I understand that as a precaution, you are keeping Central Security

Service in the dark on this. I'll leave it up to you to decide how much involvement you need from Cyber Command. Please pass on my gratitude to all those involved. Let them know as well that this is just the beginning of an enormous effort to preserve and protect the values upon which our country was founded. Everyone must continue to work hard and remain vigilant. Now, how to proceed...what is your level of confidence in the plan?"

Clausen paused before responding. "Mister President, the plan is not perfect, but it is the best my team has been able to come up with. If it weren't, I wouldn't have sent it to you. And of course, I wouldn't have sent it to you if I didn't think it could work. It is an approach derived from hundreds of thousands of beta tested iterations of a multitude of options we mapped from initiation to completion. That exercise netted us ten possible plans, each a similar variation of the other. But none had remotely as high a probability of success as the recommendation we went with. Bottom line, there are real possibilities that this initiative could fail, but no other approach would likely succeed. Even with the risks involved, doing less or nothing, or delaying action is far less attractive."

"Okay, I expected an answer like that..." the President quipped. "I found it notable there was no real contingency plan. Is there one?"

"Yes sir, there are several, depending upon the type and disposition of failure. To begin with, our exit strategy has a relatively high probability of success. On the other hand, if our primary plan fails and we decide to continue, probability of success goes down with each alternative course of action we can pivot to. In my assessment, if faced with such a situation, we will circle the wagons and discuss but would most likely withdraw versus launching any contingency plan." Clausen held his breath unconsciously, waiting for a response.

After what seemed an interminable pause, the President continued. "OK, so it sounds like this is a one-shot deal. If it fails, it fails. I do have one final question. You are recommending Mac Sisco to lead Apogee. How confident are you in his abilities? Has he done this sort of thing before? I mean, he's your top guy, right?"

Clausen responded without hesitation. "Mr. President, the team we've put together is the best in the world. Mac knows and trusts them all, so do I. They are each the best at what they do and have been doing it for years. As for Mac, he's the real deal. Everyone looks up to him. He has an uncanny ability to find the right solution for almost any challenging problem, and he does it with his head most of the time—he'll skip past the data analytics. It's what we need right now with this I think, someone who can make good, fast decisions."

"Alright Jim, I trust you with this. As a final note, and I know you already know this, but this conversation never happened. My meeting with the DNI never happened. I am completely unaware of FACET and Apogee, and there must be nothing—no email, no paper, nothing said except between me, you, and the DNI that ties me to this. Keep me apprised."

Clausen smiled. "Understood, and thank you, Mr. President."

He ended the call, replacing the gray handset in its cradle, then picked up his black internal phone and pressed the top in a vertical row of buttons. "Martin, please round up my direct reports and have them come to my office immediately, *Apogee is a go.*"

◆

"The Butterfly Effect, wow!" exclaimed Joe Franklin. "I sure hope we're not just flapping our wings on this one."

Everyone turned to look his way as he smiled broadly and comically flapped his big arms in the air.

"I'm just sayin..." he continued, "I'll bet none of you ever had a mission with such clear purpose and guidance."

The response was muted chuckles. Mac frowned. He'd just finished his opening brief and there was palpable tension all around.

Peter Singe broke through the tensity. "You sure were right Mac when you said this was Sci-Fi. But I must admit, the prep work looks good and as crazy as it sounds, it makes sense."

"I agree," Swan volunteered, "but how we execute is my concern. I presume, Mac you are now ready to share how this little team is supposed to pull off the implementation?"

From the end of the long table, Warsaw followed up, "I'm with Carrie; we may all be at the top of our game but there are only five of us. And you Mac, our fearless leader."

"Yeah, as one who has spent a lot of time on the water, this does feel a lot like trying to turn a battleship with an outboard motor," Franklin added.

They all gazed at Mac expectantly. He knew this was coming, and unfortunately, he didn't have all the answers. Not yet, anyway. "OK team, yes this one is complex, and our team is small. Just remember that we have the full weight and support of the NSA behind us. The plan has two modes of attack. One is macro, and one is micro. The code name for this approach is M&m. The Macro, or big M, exerts societal level pressure and the micro, or little m, focuses on individuals and small actions. Macro pressures will be executed by the NSA, the NSC, and POTUS and include things like international financial markets, executive and diplomatic actions, critical military repositioning, media releases, and so on. The micro actions are where our team comes in. We will be responsible for small, tactical maneuvers and pressures that are carefully coordinated in time and place and linked to the big M moves.

There was a murmur of understanding around the table. Mac noted through the three-quarter inch-thick window that the fog was just lifting over the Atlantic. The horizon had just appeared, as if by magic, and he smiled. They were all beginning to see where this was going.

"So..." Singe jumped in again. "It's kind of like when I fly my dad's CJ-4 jet. The big M actions are like the thrust of the engines pushing the aircraft forward at 600 MPH, and the small m moves are the rudder, ailerons and elevator, the tiny adjustments of which change the direction and altitude."

"Leave it to my friend Peter to turn this into an aviation class," Mac replied. "Actually, it's not a bad analogy. I would add that it's like we are flying a plane with no windows, and no instruments. All we have is a radio. The big M is also the autopilot, something we'll have to disengage from time to time so we can make our changes, but then we reengage it and wait while the upper echelon does their thing and calls to give us feedback and new directions. But make no mistake, these small, butterfly effect actions are critical to achieving the precise results we need and without them, this dog don't hunt. As they say in Texas."

Ever the comedian, Franklin couldn't help ending the meeting with another laugh. "That plane is going to be a bitch to land, I reckon."

CHAPTER EIGHT

TYPHON

Peter Gunderson listened intently as his son and Krishinko urgently described the impending crisis they had uncovered. As he relayed the details, Gunderson paced the floor in front of the bay window, much like a wild animal looking for a way out of a cage. He stopped abruptly and turned to face the two with a scowl, his eyes narrowing. Krishinko froze, waiting anxiously.

"So," Gunderson began in a low voice," if I understand correctly, we have several problems that may or may not be related that, despite all our precision and attention, we are just now discovering. Is that right?"

Krishinko nodded while trying to avoid his boss's glare. "Yes sir, it appears that way." Jefferey winced at Krishinko's idiotic choice of words.

"What do you mean, *it appears that way*, Nicholi?" Gunderson fired back. "It most definitely *is* that way." The volume of his voice rose with every word. "Apparently, we have a serious breach which we have not yet identified. Either we have a mole, or we have screwed up somewhere along the way."

He continued pacing. "But it's more than that. We are also seeing countervailing activities that could have been put in play to begin undoing some of our positions. I only noticed because there was a pattern—they seem to have happened simultaneously and I can't pinpoint the catalysts. This comes as we are also getting intelligence from sources on the ground that it appears there could be state-run countermeasures being organized against our initiatives, but we don't know who, where, what or when. I suspect it is the U.S. government. So, these are unexpected problems that we must mitigate immediately." He stopped and scowled at them again. "Or are there any other lovely surprises you would like to share?"

Jefferey winced and attempted to lower the tension in the room. "Dad, some of these activities may well be linked, but maybe not all in the way you think. And that may be a silver lining."

Gunderson's demeanor softened slightly. "What do you mean?"

"As you suspect, everything we know so far points to the U.S. intelligence community. Our sources are everywhere. FBI, CIA, DIA, even the Justice Department. They are all thoroughly infiltrated and in most, we have assets on the top floor. But as you know, we don't have anyone positioned at a high level in the NSA. Our preliminary assessment is that these efforts are originating there."

The old man grimaced. "That figures," he said flatly. "They have always been an anathema. Ever since the Snowden fiasco, their compartmentalization has been impossible to breach. That said, we do have some assets in the building."

"Yes, and we've already made the calls," Jefferey quickly added. "We should get feedback tomorrow."

The senior Gunderson was calming down. "We need to get a feel for how engaged POTUS is. If he knows nothing about it, it probably means they are unsure about the threat, that they don't have enough information yet. Or maybe even that they don't know if there's a threat at all and they are just probing."

"That will be difficult to assess," answered Jefferey. "But it's always been considered an inevitability, correct? That as long as what we've put in motion reaches the point of no return, it won't matter, right? And we are about there now."

"That is all true," chimed in Krishinko. "We will prevail."

Gunderson was nodding. "Yes, we will prevail. And yes, we did anticipate this, but not this soon. Though we have the inertia, I believe there are certain things that could happen that would derail us. For instance, if they ever found out about us, this place. If they managed to break in here, capture us alive, and get everything off our servers. But back to the regional aberrations. Are they happening because the frog jumped out of the pot or because of interventions by Washington?"

Jefferey was confused. "Dad, I'm not tracking. If the Americans were engaged, you would see efforts to shut these actions down, not exacerbate them."

Gunderson smiled like a Cheshire cat. "Not necessarily. There are two approaches. You can either slow down the boil or speed it up. Slowing it down, dampening the activities, only serves to lengthen the inevitable while mollifying the public to accept the status quo. That's what we've been doing. Speeding it up, accelerating disruption, that's a significant emotional event. The frog, or the people in this case, could react strongly in opposition. That," emphasized Gunderson, "is possibly what the Administration wants. There is a national election this November. POTUS wants to get credit for saving the country from a socioeconomic collapse."

Gunderson turned to Krishinko. "What do you think?"

Fully recovered now, he answered with confidence. "I have surveyed all twenty of our regional commissars on this and there is strong consensus that the acceleration is occurring because state leaders can't control the triggers. We always assumed we would have to prime these disruptions, but it's turned out that some of these events occur like spontaneous combustion. At this stage, it's very hard to dampen. They must be careful not to jeopardize their status by stunting organic outbreaks. It would be noticed."

"Furthermore," added Jefferey, "I don't believe we have been compromised. The CIA and the NSC are still trying to figure all this out, and to be honest their primary theory is that the whole thing is simply organic. A natural phenomenon."

Another pause, and Gunderson continued. "OK, there's no point in speculating. Let's reconvene tomorrow at 3:00 pm. I want answers with facts, not opinions."

The two answered with a curt, "yes sir," and turned to leave the room. Gunderson picked up his glass of scotch, still half full, and held it up to the light. He admired the purity of the golden liquid while reflecting on the many years that bottle waited to be opened. It was the embodiment of his family's generational quest, aged and refined over many decades. He hoped he hadn't opened it too soon.

As he drained his glass, he mentally retraced the conversation with his son and Krishinko. He agreed with the assessment but was mildly concerned about the seemingly accelerated activities. Mass demonstrations, violent public actions. They could become more frequent, larger. Unmanageable. That variable would make his work more complex and expensive, but entropy at this level was not easy to steer, even when things are going well.

He was not particularly worried about strategic intervention by the U.S. or other governments. Those reactions were inevitable and would vary from country to country. Some would push the disruption so they could appeal to the populous for more control. Others would attempt to shut it down to demonstrate the government's effectiveness and to stay in power. Some might even do it because they felt it was the right thing for the people. Gunderson couldn't help but laugh out loud at that. Either way, it didn't matter. He was confident that at this point, no matter what was done, in the end he would be in control. He will have won.

Before the Gunderson family's reign, the organization was a loose conglomeration of relationships between powerful people with likeminded values and views. As the years passed, it evolved to include elements of governments, corporations, unions, and influential and wealthy individuals with global reach. It became a global entity. It was also invisible, its operations cloaked behind legitimate structures. Indentured followers in strategic positions unwittingly belonged and furthered the cause. Money, blackmail, power plays, and threats were all used as tools to secure absolute control. Once vetted, hooked, and on the line, there was no escape. For those who knew or suspected they were part of something bigger, they didn't truly understand what it was they belonged to, only that they were proud of it and remained loyal. Those that did not were summarily ostracized, removed, ruined, and in some cases, they simply disappeared. They only ever knew their immediate controller, and most of the time that person wasn't really who they thought they were. It was a compartmented structure of the first order that, like Gunderson's fine scotch, was over twenty years in the making. The organization was multiheaded. It could survive, its mission continued if one or more high-level leaders were suddenly compromised, killed, or detained. It was perfect. This was Typhon.

Typhon's end state was Gunderson's vision, and he ruled it with an iron hand. Success was richly rewarded. Money, fame, and power were there for the taking. Failure, however, was met with swift and severe repercussions. Second chances were rare and serious missteps resulted in serious accidents. And Gunderson could never be deposed, he made sure of that. Only a very few direct reports knew who ran Typhon, and every one of them were tethered to arrangements that would end their lives, and the lives of their families if they revolted or turned on him.

Now in the home stretch, he felt uncharacteristically nervous. Their grand plan had always been to gain control of the levers of power that drove the directions of humanity, and in so doing control the people as well. Federal governments, financial markets, media, educational systems, water and food distribution, and other critical natural resources (oil, coal, lithium, copper and iron, bauxite, etcetera). There were so many and varied controls that it seemed impossible.

His forefathers had come to understand, however, that it really wasn't that complex. The real movers and shakers were often not the public leaders, but influencers with two common traits, money, and power. As the world's population exceeded eight billion, technology and globalization made these levers easier to identify and control. And Typhon had achieved terminal velocity.

So why was he feeling so nonplussed? Gunderson had always had just one nagging concern. It was almost philosophical, and that bothered him too. In every plan, particularly the complex ones, there were assumptions, and you did your best to minimize them. He had spent more time than he liked to admit pouring over every detail to eliminate them and where he couldn't, he built contingencies. Over the years, this approach had worked well but as he neared the end, there was still one that gnawed at him. If you controlled the levers of power in society, you controlled the people and ultimately how they behaved. Typhon's entire mission was built on this premise. Historically, the evidence demonstrated consistently that this approach worked on a limited scale and for a time. But it had never been proven on a global scale. If this assumption was not true, then Typhon would fail. It might be able to gain control, but it might fail in maintaining it. *But*, he said to himself angrily, *I will never let that happen.*

CHAPTER NINE

TURBULENCE

The next five days were brutal. Early hours were spent in physical training, a high intensity mix of aerobic and anaerobic workouts that was over before sunrise. Showers and breakfast followed by four hours of planning, roll playing and tactical review. After a light lunch, more operational training followed by rigorous field simulations. Equipment proficiency was part of every day's agenda, from weapons training to state-of-the-art technology platforms. Communications protocols were especially crucial. The to-do list was long and the days were short, but by liftoff they would be ready. The day before departure was committed to a final review of the overall plan, their specific assignments, and exfiltration strategies.

It was an overcast afternoon with a chance of showers as they convened one final time. Mac called the session to order as they were seated. "Ok, listen up. Tomorrow, we head out. Our targets have been mapped out and scheduled in a very specific sequence. We will adhere strictly to that. Remember that what we do is synchronized with big M. If something goes awry, the whole plan could fail."

Mac and his team walked through the details of Set One, the first of four assignments. Each was unique and would require very different outcomes. The first two were staged in the U.S., one in Chicago and one in Ruidoso, New Mexico. The next two were London and Paris.

Set One required fourteen days, after which they would reconnoiter back at Fort Meade to prepare for Set Two.

The nondescript NSA jet maneuvered carefully into the private hanger at the O'Hare FBO and coasted to a stop. The Apogee team disembarked and loaded into two black Suburbans for the forty-five-minute run into the city. Mac, Joe, and Warsaw were together in the lead vehicle with Joe at the wheel.

Warsaw was reviewing some of the possible cultural ramifications of the plan as they sped down Route 90. "Tomorrow is the last day of the National Teacher's Convention," she explained. "A series of educational policies will be debated and voted on, which if adopted will have a long-term impact on the curricula of K through 12 education across America. We are supposed to scuttle the vote, which should catalyze an existing counter movement to gain the traction it needs to reverse the fundamental direction of the nation's public primary school system. A back-to-basics renaissance, if you will."

"There are five key educators that will make or break the vote," interjected Mac. "Two are intractable and would require extraordinary pressure to change their positions. The other three are malleable but will need incentives."

◆

John Whitaker, President of the National Teacher's Union, relaxed in his suite at Chicago's Ritz-Carlton. He was looking forward to finally getting his groundbreaking, social democracy platform passed. It would cement, once and for all, the demise of school choice, crush charter schools and ensure a progressive educational agenda across the entire country. He didn't feel bad at all about the bribes, threats, and entrapments he'd orchestrated to guarantee approval. It was for the greater good. Furthermore, his lavish lifestyle and personal security would be protected. It was a major milestone in the primary commitment he made to his anonymous, like-thinking sponsor.

Whitaker stood up from the overstuffed leather chair intent on heading for the hotel bar when a knock startled him. He was not expecting anyone and had placed the *do not disturb* placard on the knob. He was a careful man by nature and carried a Glock 17 when travelling. Although Chicago's gun laws were among the most restrictive in the country, he decided to have his personal security guard bring it through airport security. He retrieved it quickly from the wardrobe and moved to the door.

With Warsaw positioned in the hotel lobby on coms, Mac and Joe rode the elevator to the eighteenth floor. They had the goods on Whitaker and the plan was simple—explain his options and convince him to flip. Mac knocked and waited.

On the other side, Whitaker was looking through the peephole. The hairs on the back of his neck began to stand up. Two men he'd never seen before in dark clothing stood just outside. His first inclination was to melt back into his suite and ignore them, but he was curious to know why they were here. He figured he could always refuse to let them in and call the front desk and hotel security. His personal security guard was probably already at the bar waiting for him.

"Who is it?" he yelled through the door.

"Mr. Whitaker, this is special agent Mac Sisco and Retired Commander Joe Franklin, may we have a minute of your time?"

Whitaker froze. Why would the IRS or FBI want anything of him? Unless they were onto his scheme. The money trail maybe... Nothing good would come of it if he didn't let them in though, so he holstered the Glock and opened the door.

As it opened, Joe and Mac got their first real look at a man who had, almost single handedly, eroded America's educational system via a propaganda machine controlled by leftist extremists. In his mid-sixties, Whitaker had all the physical characteristics of a powerful executive—tall, graying temples, angular features, and steely gray eyes. He exuded a level of confidence indicative of a man who was used to being in charge.

"Gentleman, I don't know you, but I will briefly allow you the benefit of the doubt, after you show me your credentials."

Franklin, with no formal badge, remained stoic as Mac reached into his suit breast pocket and held his NSA ID out for Whittaker to see.

"May we come in and have a few minutes of your time?" asked Mac politely as he repocketed his badge. "I assure you, it is in your best interest to hear what we have to say."

Thirty minutes later, John Whitaker's confidence was replaced by extreme anxiety. His face was ashen as he unconsciously clenched and unclenched his fists. Sisco and Franklin had methodically laid out his career of failings, falsehoods, and criminal activities. They had him on video, testimonials from witnesses, and gigabytes of text, telephone, and other documentation. Evidence of his illegal actions. The vast majority would have been inadmissible in court, but he did not know that. He was cornered with no way out, and he knew it.

When they were done showing him, he was as white as a sheet. "Um, so, um, what do you want then? I... I think I need my lawyer."

Mac immediately stepped forward, his face inches from Whitaker's and quietly whispered, "No. What you need is to switch sides and undo everything you have done. We'll make it worth your while. This is your best option, and if you don't take it, we'll get what we want anyway, and you'll go to jail."

"Um, OK, but how, do I do that?" He whined, his color beginning to come back.

"It won't be that hard," Franklin jumped in. "As we speak, in four other hotel rooms just like this one, four of your voting co-conspirators are also being flipped. In the debate leading up to the vote, you will strongly embrace a major shift in educational priorities. You will also initiate a major shift in priorities for our colleges and universities. We'll be giving you directions later on what we need you to do and say."

"Mr. Whitaker," Mac continued. "If you cooperate, we will take no action against you. If you fail to comply, you will be exposed, arrested, and found guilty and imprisoned. I would say we're being pretty generous."

Whitaker said nothing, put his head in his hands and began shaking. Finally, he looked up and said, "I guess I have no choice. I will do what I can to comply, but you should know that it is a very difficult thing you are asking me to do. First, everyone who knows me won't be able to believe it. I'll be pissing off a whole lot of people. It is career suicide. They will stop at nothing to remove me afterwards. And I fear for my life."

"What do you mean by that?" Mac asked.

Whitaker sighed. "I don't really know who they are, but they are powerful and committed to controlling the direction and future of our educational systems. And they've made it very clear that if I say anything, or if I don't do what they say..."

"Let us worry about all that," said Mac. "It's in *our* best interest to protect you. And your family. Without your help, our efforts become much more difficult. Now, we're not close to being done here, so let's order some room service. You have a lot to tell us."

The next day, they all met in the convention hall to debrief. Whitaker was good to his word, with the help of his four henchmen, each of whom had been similarly dealt with by members of Team Apogee. Even before the conference wrapped up, all of Chicago's major media headlines told of an unprecedented seismic shift in educational policy that passed late in the conference by a narrow vote.

As they all toasted the outcome at 30,000 feet on their way to New Mexico, Mac compared notes with the group. Before leaving Whitaker's suite, he and Franklin grilled Whitaker about his anonymous sponsor. All he was able to give them was a description, a name, which was undoubtedly fake, and other bits and pieces. Mac felt his adrenaline kick in as he considered the implications. It was their first real insight into who and what may be behind the conspiracy.

A sleepy mountain resort town, Ruidoso lies in the Sierra Blanca mountain range of south-central New Mexico. The quaint little village is bisected by a river by the same name, really more of a modest stream that runs adjacent to main street and meanders through the downtown. As unlikely a place as Ruidoso seemed, it was the location of the team's second most urgent target. Set Two. NSA intel identified Ruidoso as the central hub of a seemingly loose network of social media and fake news movements, operational over the last decade. The 12,000-foot Mountains offered an otherwise majestic backdrop for the surreptitious effort to control America's most influential media outlets.

James LeMaster, called Jimmy by his friends, made millions during the early growth of social media platforms. His short-lived Berkley college experience had left him angry and extreme. LeMaster was a skilled orator and communicator and quickly learned how to gain support from wealthy California radicals. His controversial digital social network, *Foulmouth*, went viral. The next several years saw even more provocative social platforms spun off from his original venture, applications that continued to provoke and inflame the most extreme factions in America. Over time, LeMaster and his backers gained more and more influence over mainstream media and became instrumental in its dramatic anti-American shifts. LeMaster's bumpy past left him with many enemies. His enclave was a fortress. Carved right into the side of a mountain and with twenty-five acres of rocky terrain falling away to the valley below, inaccessible but for a single, one-lane road with fourteen switchbacks. The perimeter of the modern 10,000-foot structure was heavily secured with electric fencing, motion detection, infrared camera systems and a roving security team twenty-four hours per day. The house was impregnable, with two-inch thick steel doors and a panic facility in the basement.

Back in Stone Harbor, there was a big debate about Set Two. The Chicago gig had gone so smoothly... The objectives had been clear, and they understood exactly how to do it. None of their targets could afford to be exposed and they were all given an escape route. Because they came up with the plan themselves, there had been no confusion, no blind spots, no problem. Set Two was a whole different ballgame. Le Master was a dangerous adversary. He had already survived several brushes with the FCC and many more within big tech who opposed him. He was surrounded by equally ruthless types who ruled by force and possessed significant financial and legal resources.

NSA had no specific tactical plan to deal with LeMaster. But their objective was clear: significantly marginalize or neutralize his entire company.

"Look," argued Curry, always quick with the financials, "there may be a way to threaten his fiscal positions such that he will agree to cease and desist on this media rampage."

"How do you propose we do that," countered Warsaw, "when his entire business plan is structured around doing just that?"

Carrie Swan interjected, "I agree with you Pat, it could be effective to threaten his income streams and resources. I think there might be a way to do that, but it's tricky. The Agency provides us with quite a bit of technical detail about the layout of his residence and the computing and network infrastructure. They hacked his systems. Not completely but enough, and we know he maintains servers in his house with all his data, including financials. If we can get into his compound and access his servers directly, I believe I may be able to get access and take control of his funds. That would give us the leverage we need to back him into a corner."

"Conceptually, this sounds good," Mac responded, "but there are a few hurdles we have to get over to make it work. One, we have no warrant. It's illegal. It will be a complete shitshow if we are caught—he's an American citizen and we don't have anything on him. But I'm willing to take the chance if the plan is airtight. Clausen didn't outright give us that type of latitude, but he did say we could bend the rules if needed. Peter, how do you think we can get through security and into the residence without anyone noticing?"

Peter sighed. "I was afraid you were going to ask me that. Believe it or not, the perimeter security is not particularly overwhelming. To get in, we'll have to shut down all electronic surveillance simultaneously, and do it in such a way that they still appear to be functioning. Then we must get through the front door, inside, access the system, and leave without anyone from his security team noticing.

"So," said Mac, "it's possible?"

"Well, I need to check on a few details with our friends back at Fort Meade, but I think we can pull it off," Peter confirmed.

Mac turned to Warsaw. "Elaine, what do you think?"

She didn't answer immediately, holding up a finger as if to say *give me a minute* as she rapidly tapped her iPad. Finally, she looked up. "Mac, I've been digging into this guy's profile, his past, his business practices and partners and every ounce of personal data we have on him, including his childhood, and I have little doubt he is a classic paranoid sociopath. That means he is very unpredictable. As a result, everything we do will be more complicated and riskier. He could surprise us at every turn, and his defenses could be more robust than they appear."

"OK. That means we must be perfect. And we cannot make any assumptions along the way. And we need a contingency plan," Mac answered.

Franklin nodded. "Yep, and there is only one option for that, we'd have to take him out!"

Everyone looked at him at once in surprise. But there was no objection...

CHAPTER TEN

COUNTERMEASURES

Peter Gunderson was up early after a restless night. True to his disciplined nature, he donned his running gear and headed downstairs ready to rip off a quick 10K before facing the challenges he knew the day would bring. He entered the sprawling kitchen, a Thermidor commercial gas stove and two double sized stainless subzero refrigerators occupying most of the far wall. Opening the subzero was like entering a bank vault as he retrieved some strawberries, blueberries, and orange juice. From a basket on the counter, he pulled and peeled a banana and in minutes the Vita-mix blender completed its work. He gulped down the smoothie as he left through the back entrance and the long shadows of an early morning sunrise. After five minutes of stretching, he was on his way down the gently sloping crushed granite trail that meandered through the property. He appreciated the crisp morning air, replete with notes of rose petals and sawgrass. The silence was intermittently broken by the chirping of robins and finches and an occasional woodpecker drumming in the distance.

"This is not good," Krishinko reported in the kitchen as he poured his second cup of steaming black coffee.

"No, it's worse than that," Jefferey said. "The old man is going to shit when he gets back from his run."

"I doubt he knows about Chicago yet," Krishinko responded. "He always works out before he does anything else. He never breaks the pattern."

"It's superstition," Krishinko agreed.

"You think *what's* a superstition?" Peter Gunderson yelled as he strode through the door.

Already caught, Jefferey quickly responded, trying to minimize any damage. "Your morning workout. We were saying that you are superstitious about it because you never miss it."

Gunderson shrugged. "You may be right." He poured himself a coffee. "So, what do we know?"

He listened attentively to the details of the Chicago situation. "What do we know from our Chicago handler, and for that matter, from any of our other sources?" he asked impatiently.

"Whitaker was coerced by some heavies he said were government agents," answered Jefferey. "They had everything on him and his four colleagues. He said he had no choice, and this was the best option, because exposure would have killed any chance he had of ever turning this back around. He also says now he can work subtly to thwart the Feds. Double agent."

Gunderson smirked. "Whitaker always was a silver-tongued devil."

"What do *you* think Mr. Gunderson?" Krishinko queried.

"Well shit, Nicholi, I can tell you that Mr. Whitaker and his friends are now removed from this initiative. We were almost there…But they are spoiled goods now, and a significant risk. Interrogate them quietly. Then they need to die of natural causes. A boating accident, car crash on the way to dinner, something like that. Make sure they're iron clad accidental deaths and try to get it done as soon as possible. It would be better to kill two or more birds with one stone—a gas explosion at a restaurant or whatnot. We've done these before. You know the drill."

"What else," Gunderson moved on dispassionately.

"We have heard nothing yet from the NSC," Krishinko responded. "Our source there says there is so much heat that any move would be very risky. Unfortunately, we're going to have to let that one simmer for a while. None of our NSA sources are directly involved with the action there, but there is a rumor of a major new initiative underway. A lot of major technical resources have been pulled off important endeavors and reassigned, all at once. And the Director, Clausen, apparently blocked his calendar for the next thirty days and has had several blue seal-level meetings recently."

Gunderson stepped over to the coffee maker and poured another cup. He looked at his son expectantly.

The younger Gunderson took his hint. "I think we called it right yesterday. Everything we now know continues to point to two scenarios that are in play. Government action that implies they have knowledge of our activities, and a new issue with our disruption strategy. And," Jefferey went on, "we suspect the NSA has a team operating against us."

Gunderson's attention focused on both men. "What are your recommendations for our immediate short-term actions?"

Once again, his son took the lead. "It is clear to me there are two moves we should make. Get the accelerated disruptions under control to protect our timeline, and to avoid public backlash. Second, we must find out who is involved with the NSA team and deal with them appropriately. They will be investigating Typhon aggressively, each action they take puts them closer to identifying who we are. I recommend Nicholi and I mobilize our resources. I will focus on the east coast, New York, Washington, D.C. Chicago, Minneapolis, and Portland are where the disruptions are also most advanced. Nicholi can take on London, Paris, Tehran, and Hong Kong. I'll spend the next couple of days on intelligence gathering to try to ID the NSA team members, see what they are doing and where they are going next. Once I know who any of them are, I'll apprehend them, interrogate them, and then terminate them."

Gunderson could not help but smile. *The apple didn't fall far.* Loyal, passionate, ruthless. *Perfect.* "Gentleman, good report, and your recommendations are sound. I agree with the plan, and I authorize its implementation immediately. Remember, Typhon is everything. Our mission must be fulfilled."

CHAPTER ELEVEN

Assault

The sun set quickly on the Sierra Blanca Mountains as the team positioned itself across the valley from LeMaster's base. As Mac observed his team, he could almost see the adrenaline pulsing through their veins. This is what they trained for. Each was equipped with active engagement tradecraft gear. A Kevlar vest, night vision optics, utility belt with lock pics, cutter, med pack and an assortment of weapons. An eight-inch tactical knife, taser, tranquilizer gun, and two semi-automatic silenced handguns with green laser sights were standard issue. While it was up to each individual on the make and model, the primary weapon was required to be a .45 caliber or a 9mm with a twenty-round magazine. Mac's choices were the tried-and-true 9mm Sig Sauer P226 Tacops and the very accurate 9mm H&K P30 with a low pull trigger. If things got rough, Joe Franklin and Pat Curry hefted POF 415 ARs with two thirty-round Magtech magazines. Everyone wore black face paint and dark patterned camo fatigues with military attack boots.

"Ok everyone, sunset in ten minutes. Then we move," Mac advised. "We will be 100 yards from the perimeter fifteen minutes later. Radio silence unless absolutely necessary. We know there are six security guards outside, and four more inside the complex, but there could be more. Any questions?"

Silence from the team meant everyone was ready to go. "Ok," Mac continued, "as soon as we breach the perimeter fence, we will confirm positions, then enter the house. If you encounter resistance, neutralize. Deadly force is authorized as required, but initial action should be non-lethal. Use your tasers or tranq darts if possible. There is no evidence of canines, but heads up anyway. Once inside, you're on your own to execute your op. Peter will work access for Swan into the Server Farm and assist her in breaking the firewall security and hacking LeMaster's funds. Joe and I will take up positions to counter any interference on the inside. Pat, you and Elaine will find LeMaster, disarm him if necessary, and deliver the ultimatum. If he gives you trouble, tell me and Joe and I will assist. He scanned each member for questions. "Ok, let's rock and roll!"

Fifteen minutes later the team assembled near the perimeter and covered the last hundred yards without incident. The motion detectors, cameras, and sensors had to be taken out all at once, followed by the breach and reactivation of the system, all within one minute. The outage was to be camouflaged as a natural 'glitch in the system.'

Peter had come up with the answer. Each surveillance system was powered independently, with auto reset breakers to bring them back online in the event of a power outage or surge, not an uncommon occurrence up in the mountains. Killing the power to all systems at once would make it appear to be such a surge. Anyone monitoring a system would simply wait for it to come back online.

Mac gave the signal and almost immediately Franklin indicated it was done. They'd already cut through the steel mesh fence, a neat three-by-five-foot opening. They silently scrambled through, advancing to cover by a grove of birch trees. Floodlights illuminated the modern steel and glass structure. Two security guards walked toward each far corner of the building, disappearing, then replaced by others following at regular intervals. Two more were stationed on terraces off the second floor, scanning the grounds for any sign of trouble. It would be easy enough to take the second-floor sentries out with the scoped ARs, but Mac wanted to minimize their exposure for as long as possible. He signaled Singe to join him behind a large bush.

"I want to tranq those guys on the second floor. Do you think you can scale that downspout on the corner, when the guards clear, and ambush them up top?" Mac asked hopefully.

One of Singe's many talents was rock climbing. "No problem, Cap," he exclaimed grinning.

"We'll create a small diversion if necessary, to move them off to the east side," Mac said.

"Copy that," Peter said as he moved off.

Mac shared the plan with the rest of the team, and they all watched anxiously as Singe crept forward. He waited patiently behind a large crepe myrtle until both guards turned the corner. Then he sprinted to the downspout via a route outside line of sight from the guards above. It was impressive how quickly he scaled the pipe. Peeking over as he arrived at the top, he waited. Curry positioned himself by the opposite end, below the terraces and gently lobbed a small rock into the shadows. It made a muted sound, not unlike a small animal scrabbling away from some unknown danger. Both guards reacted as predicted and cautiously advanced together to peer over the railing on that side. Peter made it over the railing and to the far end of the terrace in an instant. He hit the nearest guard with a dart, who collapsed immediately. The second, now facing him and reaching for his weapon, grabbed at his neck as a second shot hit him. His AK-47 clattered to the terrazzo, followed quickly by the rest of him as the fast-acting tranquilizer did its thing. Singe dragged them both out of sight and melted back into the shadows as quickly as he had appeared.

The guards were due to appear momentarily. Mac raised his hand and made a silent signal to move forward. Singe slid down the gutter spout and ran to a position near the entrance. As the first sentry appeared around the corner, he caught Peter's movement. Astonished at seeing an intruder, he froze, and then reached for his radio to sound the alarm. Mac saw all this in slow motion and for just a second, he thought they might be exposed. Then the guard crumpled to the ground. Franklin retrieved his radio and weapon before dragging the unconscious man into the nearby trees. Moments later, the next two guards rounded opposite corners and were dispatched with tranqs. Five down, one to go on the outside. Things were going well so far.

Mac moved behind the house while the team was handling the last guard. Then he realized something was wrong. That last guard was not coming back. He crept forward, his NVGs off now as his eyes acclimated to the floodlights. He heard a faint tinkling sound off to his right, away from the house. As he peered out from behind another large decorative bush, he saw and heard the guard moaning softly, relieving himself into a small patch of prickly cacti. He collected himself, then walked back towards the residence.

Mac waited in the shadows, his taser at the ready. As the guard passed a mere six feet from him, he stepped out and aimed it at his back and pulled the trigger. But nothing happened… He activated it again, again nothing. Sensing his motion, the big guard spun around, stepping into a combat stance while raising his AK.

A long-barreled weapon is less effective in close quarters. If he were well trained, the guard should expect Mac to rush him. Mac moved in at him, low and fast, diving under the guard's arms and below the AK. There wasn't enough time for the man to track him with the weapon, much less pull the trigger. Mac impacted the man at his knees while sweeping his left arm forcefully, up and over the AK, ripping it from his grasp. Mac noted the strike point and inertia of his defensive move were just right as he felt and heard tendons and cartilage pop and tear. The AK flew from his hands, its trigger never pulled, and he groaned in pain while crumbling backwards to the ground.

Mac popped up, sensing a gash on his left shoulder from a sharp rock. He shrugged it off and zip tied the man's hands and feet, then gagged him with a strip of cloth ripped from his own shirt. He debated a quick interrogation. Hearing footsteps approaching, he grabbed for his Sig. "Whoa, boss," Franklin cautioned, "it's just me."

Mac lowered his Sig. "Right. I was about to interrogate this guy about the inside set up, but I'm not sure we have time."

Franklin smiled, reached down and helped Mac to his feet, then immediately shot a tranq dart into the guard's chest. "Sorry. We need to go *now*. These guys check in regularly and we've got to get inside before they know they have a problem. Someone may have heard the commotion."

Singe had his gear out and was working on the front door. He glanced over as Mac approached with Franklin, noting the blood staining his shoulder.

"It's just a scratch," Mac dismissed. "You should see the other guy. Almost done, Peter?"

"The locking mechanism is complex. But the more complex something is, the more ways there are to attack it." He was attaching an electronic device to the keypad.

Swan looked perturbed. "Occam's razor," she offered.

Peter looked up, irritated at being interrupted. "What?"

"Occam's razor," she repeated. "The simplest answer is most likely the correct one."

Singe now looked confused as Swan reached over, grabbed the handle, depressed the latch, and pulled the heavy door open.

Mac rolled his eyes as Singe quickly stuffed his gear back in his bag, and they all went inside.

They fanned out immediately. Franklin and Mac took up positions on opposite ends of the large foyer. From there, three corridors led away to the rest of the expansive structure. While they stood watch, the rest of the team searched the building.

In planning, they had budgeted fifteen minutes to locate LeMaster and his computer center, so Mac was surprised when Swan was back on comms after less than five.

"Mac," she said, "we have a problem."

"Explain," he replied.

"The servers have been removed. The racks are gone."

"Shit," he whispered forcefully. "How could they have known we were coming?"

Pat Curry cut in. "Mac, we have a bead on LeMaster. He and several guards are fleeing the second floor. We caught a glimpse of them going down a stairway at the end of the hall from his private quarters."

"Do they have the servers with them?" Mac shot back.

"Not that I could tell," Curry replied.

"Pat, you and Elaine stay in pursuit, but be careful. Follow at a distance and keep us apprised of their movements. Carrie and Pete— see if there's anything that might indicate where the servers were taken. We're going up top to head them off. Joe, you take the south side, I'll take the north."

Then the lights went out, and all hell broke loose. At first, there was dead silence as he and Franklin rushed outside. And then Mac heard it, faintly at first but growing in volume. A low growl, guttural and angry bounced off the walls making it hard to know where it came from. Mac turned on his night vision goggles and flipped them down over his eyes. The eerie greenish glow made him feel like he was trapped in another dimension and the growing feral noises now seemed to be coming from several directions.

"Joe, status?" he whispered.

"I have company."

"What kind of company?" Mac asked.

"Dogs," came his reply.

"Same here," Mac said. "Stay vigilant everyone—if you see one, just shoot it."

Mac then saw them round the corner, two. Within a second, they were nearly on him. Huge Belgian Malinois, trained to attack intruders. They leapt forward together, ears pinned back and accelerating towards him. Mac heard six reports from Franklin's location in quick succession as he fired his own handgun at the two dogs, now launched midair and just feet away.

He couldn't avoid them and wasn't sure he'd hit them both before they were on him. He feinted right to miss the first and absorbed the bone crushing impact of the second an instant later. He flew backwards with the animal on top of him onto the grass, coming to rest next to the writhing animal. Mac's right leg was folded unnaturally beneath him. He winced as he tried to stand. *A sprain.*

"Joe, status!"

Nothing.

He limped over to the far corner of the building and saw him, a greenish glowing figure sprawled on the ground between to unmoving canines. Blood was pooling around his head. Mac knelt beside him and checked his pulse and breathing, then applied pressure to the gash on his neck.

"Team, check in." Mac commanded.

"Elaine and I are still following the target, they took an elevator to a lower level—heading to the stairs in pursuit," Curry came back.

"Mac, this is Carrie, still in the server room. Not having much luck finding any clues about the servers."

"Carrie, Joe and I were attacked by dogs, Joe is down and needs medical assistance immediately."

"We are down in a sub-level. Peter will stay on them, give me a few minutes."

Forty seconds passed. Followed closely by Singe, Swan emerged running through the front door, med kit in-hand, and began working on Franklin. The big man's eyes start to flutter, and he muttered almost incoherently, "Wha happen?"

"Take it easy Joe, I got you," Swan reassured as she finished bandaging his neck. He came around quickly. She checked his pupils with a pen light and determined he was good to go.

"What about you, you OK?" Swan asked Mac.

"Sprained knee. Nothing I can do about it right now."

"OK. What now?" she asked.

"Let's head back in and find Pat and Elaine." Mac responded, helping Franklin to his feet.

Curry and Warsaw followed LeMaster and his goons down one corridor after another in the massive underground space. Their night vision gear was effective, but not perfect. They still required a minimum level of ambient light to work well. Even with infrared enhancement, objects at a distance were often indistinct. The good news was, their quarry had no such advantage and were using flashlights, which made them very easy to follow.

As they came to yet another juncture with two additional corridors, there was a thud as a live round chipped the concrete wall just twelve inches in front of Warsaw's head. She jerked backwards instinctively, bumping into Curry. They both crouched low and moved slowly backwards into the corridor. Curry contemplated tossing flashbang grenades around the corner. They waited silently for several seconds, then heard the dull thud of a door closing at the end of the adjacent hall.

Cautiously, they peered around the corner. Seeing it was empty, they advanced slowly toward the massive door. There was no handle. Two biometric devices were mounted on the wall to the left. One for a fingerprint scan, and one for a facial scan.

"I'm impressed, you don't even see that in banks." Pat stated resignedly.

"Well, I told you this guy is certifiable," quipped Warsaw.

Then she keyed her radio. "Mac, we're at a dead-end. Biometric locks on a door. I'll talk you down to us."

"Copy that," came back the reply. "We're at the stairwell now."

♦

Jimmy LeMaster knew intruders had breached his residence as soon as the front door remained unlocked for more than thirty seconds. A modestly loud alarm woke him from a deep sleep. The pattern and tone of the alarm told him what the emergency was. Every type of breach had its own signal.

Once an alarm was triggered, automated lockdown procedures commenced, and his security team was trained to follow specific protocols for each type of alarm. A guard was in his chamber within seconds and briefed him. These appeared to be professionals and there were an unknown number of them in his home. Several guards were down.

Following their protocols, part of his team disconnected the servers while others escorted him to safety. His priority for escape was to flee in armored vehicles from the garage. Along the way, they released the dogs to slow the intruders, maybe even take a few out.

Enroute to the garage, however, their escape route was blocked. So, they opted for Plan B, the safe room. With sleeping quarters, a kitchen, computer and communications connectivity and enough food and air for six to last an entire year, they could wait out any form of threat.

Once inside, he quickly booted his computers and turned on his communications equipment. He needed to understand who might be behind the attack, then determine his best course of action. The local police were his preference, but he had to be careful. There were things in his mountain home, secrets he didn't want anyone to know about. If he could handle it himself, he may choose to do that. He kept an elite, private team on call for just that eventuality. One text and a within an hour a helicopter would swoop in and this whole thing would be over very quickly. He could then take the next few hours to assess the potential fallout and how best to proceed. *Either way*, he thought to himself, *no one messes with Jimmy LeMaster.*

When they were all at the safe room door, the atmosphere was somber. It was going so well, and then things went to shit. Not only had they taken some hits, but LeMaster was behind an impregnable door, probably along with his servers. The mission was in serious jeopardy, and they all knew it. It might only be an hour or less before local authorities were on the scene.

As they considered their options, Mac reminded them that they had some clean up to do. The guards would soon be recovering. Zip tied and gagged, they wouldn't be able to do much but should be at least dragged into the house. One by one they carried the security team to a supply room in the residence and locked them securely inside. The dogs were dragged back to the kennel and stashed inside. They collected the guards' weapons and communications gear, placing it all in a pile on the main floor living room. Then they locked the facility securely, cut all power and communication lines to the compound, and met in the foyer to discuss next steps.

"I know we're all tired and frustrated, but there is a silver lining," Mac explained. "He's holed up, but he can't go anywhere, and we are still all in one piece."

"Yeah OK," said Franklin. "Not to be a pessimist, though, but the clock is running. We don't know what resources he has in that safe room. For all we know, he's already called the police and they're almost here. Or worse, he has a team inbound to take us out."

Warsaw chimed in. "His only option is to call the police. He doesn't know who we are, but he's probably stressed right now about how serious this is—he had good defenses but never expected a government agency to blow in SWAT-style. My guess is he hasn't brought the police in yet because he suspects that may only complicate things for him—and it would. He's trying to figure out who we are and why we are here. The more time we give him, the more difficult it may be to get what we need."

"You're all right," Mac agreed. "We need to either get into that room or convince him to come out."

After some analysis and reconnoitering, they determined there was only the one entry into the safe room. They also suspected it was soundproof and hermetically sealed, all of which limited their options. They would need a heavy-duty concrete drill and pneumatic jack hammer or an industrial steel cutter to force their way in, which they didn't have.

While Singe and Swan brainstormed options, Warsaw briefed Mac and Curry on a totally different angle. "I think we can exploit him psychologically."

"I'm intrigued," Mac replied. "Go on."

"So," she continued, "We have a thorough workup on him, and I studied it. I also reached out to the FBI. I was surprised they even had a file on him, but they did, and they sent it to me. There's a lot in it I think we can work with."

"Like what?" Mac asked.

"Well, he was physically abused by his father, who was a drunk. His mother left him with LeMaster and moved to California, but father eventually found them and tried to re-assert himself. By that time, LeMaster was an adult. Shortly after the father showed up, he disappeared. The Bureau thinks LeMaster killed him and hid the body, but the evidence was circumstantial. Anyway, his mother is still alive, now in her 70's, and living in San Diego under another name. Records show she is supported financially through an offshore shell corporation that can be traced back to LeMaster. We might be able to use this information to get him to comply."

The team reassembled and they reviewed their options. They agreed there were only two that had any chance of success and within the limited time they had left. One, convince LeMaster's mother to tell him she would be at risk if he didn't comply. Or two, figure out a way to fool the sensor system and open the vault door. Neither approach was ideal, so they decided to try both in parallel. They would execute whichever worked first and discontinue with the other. Warsaw and Curry took the mother angle, and Singe and Swan turned the power back on and began working on the sensors. Mac and Franklin posted in a second-floor room with a large window giving them a sweeping view of the grounds. They kept watch while outlining how each scenario should successfully play out, and what the contingencies should be if both failed.

A short while later, Warsaw came on Mac's earpiece. "Mac, we hit a dead end with his mother. I was unable to reach her via phone, so I had a local agent swing by her place. She's not there, and apparently evidence in the house suggests she packed quickly and left. She's in the wind."

"Well, shit," Mac replied. "I hope Peter and Carrie are having better luck."

"Still working it Mac," Swan cut in. "All this will be for nothing, though, if there is a biometric lockout inside the saferoom. We have no way to know. Both scanners are still powered though."

Mac turned to Franklin, "My bet is that he has already made a call and whoever they are, they're on the way. We need to move now."

He cued his mic again. "Elaine, get Pat and meet us in the comm center. Either we're ready for option two or we'll have to withdraw and regroup."

Singe and Swan were online with the NSA to research the sensor problem. They'd given them photos of each, the manufacturer names, model numbers, and other pertinent information. By the time everyone was together in the comm center, they were finishing up the call pouring over a detailed wiring blueprint displayed on Swan's iPad.

Singe looked up at the team. "So, here's the deal. We can't disable the locks. We can't get to the wiring, and we can't hack the sensors because the primary logic is hardwired to prevent just that. To make matters worse, they must be used in a specific order, or they won't open the door, and both will become inoperative for a programmed amount of time—which we don't know. It could be a minute, an hour, a day... We need to know which one to active first."

"Well, we're screwed then," Franklin exclaimed.

"Maybe not," Swan offered, "but we must get it right the first time. If we get everything right but blow the sequence and get locked out, we could be out of options."

"Now we know what we can't do," Warsaw continued, "but first things first, how do we trick the sensors?"

All eyes were on Swan and Singe.

Swan began. "The NSA sent us an app loaded with high-res images of LeMaster's face from thousands of angles. He's all over the internet, so that was easy. The hard part is making the sensor think a flat screen is three-dimensional, and that is what the app does."

She held up her iPad and moved it in various directions. The photo took on a three-dimensional look as she moved the screen, as if his head were literally inside the device.

"We must hold the iPad in front of the sensor and rotate it thirty degrees in each direction vertically, then horizontally. That's supposed to do the trick. For the second scanner, all I needed was his index fingerprint, which I lifted off the scanner itself. I have a kit with me that will fabricate a print emulation, which you basically just stick on your own finger. We use these all the time, and I suspected we might need it to access his servers."

Franklin nodded. "Well, that's easy enough."

"We still need to do them in the right order, though. And that, unfortunately will be nothing but an educated guess," Swan cautioned.

"I assume you have a theory?" Curry asked.

"Yes, we do. The scanners are situated on the wall vertically, the facial scanner above the fingerprint scanner," Peter explained. "If you are trying to get in quickly, you would want to be able to do it as fast as possible. Both at the same time would be fastest, but that's not the setup. The fingerprint scanner is nearly instantaneous, but the facial recognition takes more time, and sometimes needs to be repeated depending on how far away you are, how tired you look on a particular day, etcetera. Because of how they integrate, if facial is programmed to be done first, you would have to repeat both scans if the facial recognition fails—but if the fingerprint scan is supposed to be done first, and facial fails, you can just repeat the facial scan until it is accepted *without* repeating the whole sequence. Because of this, I think it makes sense that the fingerprint scan is first."

"I'm interested in what Elaine thinks based on his psych profile," Singe added.

"OK, well…" Warsaw began. "He's paranoid and egomaniacal, but I don't think either thing factors. He's also very smart and logical. He would go with the most efficient solution."

The tension seemed to melt away as their confidence grew that they could still pull the mission off.

"Well, that's it then, let's do it," Mac said.

Their hope was LeMaster was overconfident in the impregnability of the saferoom, that they'd catch him and his thugs off guard. They'd already disabled the camera and microphone above the door, so hopefully they were unaware of what Mac and his team were planning. Singe and Swan would manage the scans. Mac and Franklin would enter as soon as the door opened. Curry and Warsaw were in position to provide backup.

Singe was ready with the printed fingerprint applied to his index finger. He placed it against the scanner. A green light appeared on the console. One down, two to go. He nodded to Swan, and she carefully positioned the iPad in front of the facial scanner, tilting it vertically, then horizontally. There was a soft purring noise as the scanner did its thing. The light below the scanner burst on brightly in a vibrant green. They all stood transfixed, not knowing exactly what would happen. Five, then ten seconds went by and suddenly a muted click sounded as if an internal switch had been thrown. Another couple seconds, and the unmistakable low grind of massive gears could be heard as the internal screw drives pulled the steel rods inward and pneumatic cylinders pushed open the massive door.

They moved forward into a narrow, dimly lit hallway with weapons at the ready. Mac and Franklin followed Swan and Singe in staggered order. Just up ahead, the hallway branched left and right, and Singe raised his fist silently for all to stop.

Peering cautiously around the corner, Mac could see two opposing, identical closed doors. Mac gave the hand signal to stay put as he considered the layout. Both the left and right hallways dead-ended and turned ninety degrees to the right and left twenty feet further up.

This is much more than just a safe room, Mac thought. "Stay vigilant. They are here somewhere, and we don't want to be caught off guard," he whispered to the team.

They moved down the left hallway first, opening each door swat-style and clearing every space. They found only an empty kitchen, dining area, and three rooms serving as sleeping quarters. In the first, Mac found a few loose sheets of scrawled notes off one of the beds. He folded the papers and put them in his tactical vest breast pocket. The other two were empty. A fourth door was locked. A faint line of light emanated from below the door.

Mac pointed at Franklin, then at Warsaw and motioned for them to guard the door. Then he, Swan, and Singe doubled back silently to the opposite hallway.

At the end and through the first door, Mac shone his flashlight across a large room stacked with big steel racks on the opposite wall. A soft glow was dimly visible on an adjacent table, fronted by several webbed office chairs. He flicked the light switch, illuminating six wide maple tables, two each against three of the walls. Each table held a large flat panel display fronted by wireless keyboards. Examining the steel racks, he counted at least five tower-style servers, several blinking modems, network routers, stacked multi-terabyte hard drives and battery backup power supplies. LeMaster's network nerve center. *Jackpot.*

Singe and Swan got to work on the consoles. Mac guarded the door and pulled the notes from his breast pocket, scanning them quickly. "Uh, oh," he muttered. "It looks like company might be on the way. There is a list of names here, with phone numbers and ETAs. I have a feeling Jimmy Boy called in some reinforcements. Let's finish up here as quickly as possible."

So far, luck had been on their side. LeMaster and his henchmen were likely holed up in that fourth bedroom. They needed to have him in custody, to use as leverage, before his backup arrived.

Mac was getting nervous—he knew they were running out of time, and it had already taken far longer than they'd planned. "Joe, any movement in that room?"

"Negative, though there's definitely someone inside. They know we're here," came the hushed reply.

"Understood," said Mac. "They're sitting tight, waiting for reinforcements. We're in the comms room now. Hopefully we'll have eyes on the premises soon. Keep me apprised."

"Copy."

Mac looked at Swan. "I'm going to go check the last door while you..."

"Gotcha!" Swan exclaimed.

"What?"

"I have access to all the cameras inside and outside the complex."

"Good." Mac walked over to her. "What are we looking at? Can we see inside that locked room?"

"Yup—there they are." She pointed to one of nine feeds on the screen in front of her. LeMaster was sitting on a bed, looking worried. Four armed guards stood at the ready, two to either side.

"Joe, LeMaster and four guards are inside that room. Looks like each are armed with a handgun and assault rifle. They are all wearing body armor."

"Copy," Franklin came back again quietly.

Singe sat down in front of the display next to her to monitor for activity on the complex grounds. Then Swan moved to another and began evaluating how to break into LeMaster's files.

♦

The two Sikorsky S-76D helicopters flew low over the Sierra Blanca Mountains. Following the rugged ridges of the New Mexico range, they throttled back to 140 knots. Each carried ten mercenaries from LeMaster's security headquarters in El Paso, Texas. They were an elite team; most were former Special Operations soldiers. Precisely two hours had elapsed since LeMaster's call from the compound.

Now, thirty minutes into their flight, they were running through the operational details and doing a final gear check. Touchdown was in less than twenty minutes. The formation would separate ten miles out and approach from opposite directions. Once on the ground, each team was to advance in two-man squads. They were nervous. Their orders included using lethal force if necessary. A few were uncomfortable with that, though their team leader had assured them it was legal—they were all licensed to perform this work and state law allowed for lethal force in defense of a home or business.

Some were confident, almost cocky, aching for some real action after being on call for weeks, even months at a time without ever getting the call. The number of assailants was small, and although they'd successfully breached the perimeter and facility, it was probable they were just professional thieves without any real combat training.

They came in opposite each other, noses down, hard and fast. Their four huge blades clawed the thin air, sending dust and debris flying. Just as the 7,000-pound machines touched their wheels to the rocky terrain, they jumped out and, crouching low, sprinted towards the compound two-by-two.

CHAPTER TWELVE

THE FROG

New York was an old friend to Jefferey Gunderson. After five years practicing international law in Manhattan, he knew the city and its mover and shakers. He knew where all the skeletons were buried. His father had convinced him to practice in New York, primarily because it was the epicenter of Typhon's assault. Strong leftist leanings and weak state and city government leadership made it particularly easy to manipulate. It had been almost child's play to establish influence within the power structure.

He focused first on municipal and state governance, then the top Wall Street firms. Mainstream media followed the money like puppies after a treat. Academia was already on his leash, succumbing almost instantly as they gobbled up strategically drafted grants like an addict desperate for a next fix. Following a Marxist playbook and Alinsky's rules to accelerate disruption, he'd catalyzed protests on a regular basis in Manhattan, some that were turning ugly. Almost every night, the city was literally assaulting itself. Riots, robberies, attacks on businesses and citizens—a myriad of convenient causes seemed to bubble up from nowhere, rapidly metastasizing into a cancerous cancellation of culture.

Jefferey smiled cautiously. *Everything is going according to plan, except...* Things were escalating too fast. Typhon's plan needed a graduated progression. They never foresaw that an accelerant might be introduced, whether it was natural or artificial. One that could quicken the maelstrom. He needed to attenuate it. So, Jefferey spent a few days before his trip to the Big Apple studying successful historical uprisings and found they shared one important commonality. In every case, the main organization driving it rapidly gained power and resources, which incentivized them to add fuel to the flames. Jefferey could control them to a certain extent by limiting funding or by empowering their adversaries. If he didn't act quickly, however, the blaze might just become self-sustaining.

Jefferey maintained a cover that allowed him limited, but secure access to most of the key players in Typhon's ground operations. He adopted a persona as an anonymous financier with access to significant funding and global reach. The best lie is close to the truth, and aside from intent, all other parts of his story were essentially true. While in the city, he planned to observe the disruptions firsthand to understand how they were being managed. Then, he needed to speak with whoever was running the show.

As dusk crept over the Manhattan skyline, Jefferey arrived at the location of today's planned protest. Hundreds had already filed into the streets carrying placards and homemade shields. Some in shorts and sandals, others in combat boots with fatigues. They marched irregularly, up and down Fifth Avenue. Blaring bullhorns and chanting filled the air in a near-meaningless cacophony.

Out of nowhere, a fireball flew through the air, shattering a shop window and quickly exploding within the building. The crowd roared approval. Soon, other windows were shattered with bricks and two by fours. Almost immediately, placards were dropped to the street as some invaded the now breached shops to loot and pillage. Some of those not participating held up their cell phones to video the ongoing destruction. Jefferey had seen enough and turned to leave with a frown of concern. The point of no return was fast approaching.

Thirty minutes later, he entered a nondescript tavern on a side street. The meeting was scheduled two days earlier, but the location was not set until earlier that afternoon. Jefferey didn't look much like a financier in his jeans, leather jacket and sneakers, but of course that was the point. He arrived a few minutes early and took a seat at a corner table in the back with a clear view of the entrance. He ordered a Guinness and waited.

As his beer arrived, a tall black man entered the bar, stopped just inside, and scanned the room. His noticed Jefferey and the half empty Guinness bottle, then made his way over and sat down without a word. He was a big, powerful man, probably six three and two-twenty. He was wearing black sweatpants, tight at the ankles, and a loose-fitting grey hoody. Dreadlocks, a goatee, and piercing dark eyes completed the intimidating picture.

The man spoke. "You're interested in making an investment."

"Yes, that's true," Jefferey answered.

"Why?" the big man questioned.

"I represent several different groups with very significant resources who have an interest in supporting groups like yours," Jefferey Responded.

"Why?" The man repeated.

"They believe your objectives are aligned with theirs."

The man in the hoodie leaned forward menacingly. "What are their objectives?"

"They believe the changes you desire will support their economic needs in this country. They feel the current policies and leadership against which you protest need to be changed."

The man seemed to relax a bit and leaned back. "What kind of dust are we talking about?"

"What do you need?" Jefferey shot back slyly.

The man's demeanor changed, and he looked upward and to the left as he contemplated a figure. "A million. To start."

"To start? For what? And what happens after that?" Jefferey asked.

Leaning forward again, the man whispered, "A million to tear it down, and a lot more afterwards to keep it the way we want it kept."

Jefferey rubbed his chin, then stared deep into the big man's eyes. "I can commit to the appetizer today."

"And the rest?" came the quick response.

"The entree is above my pay grade. I'll need some time."

The big man frowned cautiously. "How long will that take?"

"Not long, a couple days probably," Jefferey said, smiling back.

"OK. One condition," the big man said. "No interference. We do things our way."

Jefferey's smile widened. "We wouldn't have it any other way."

As Jefferey drove his big Mercedes down the New Jersey turnpike, he mused about all he had learned over the last few hours. Things were near the breaking point. The ferocity and violence of riots everywhere were increasing, and in a seemingly geometric manner. Even with the media consistently misrepresenting them as peaceful protests, the public was catching on.

The meeting proved fruitful in that regard, illuminating a number of crucial details. Though it was essentially a single data point, his theory of acceleration appeared to be valid. And the big man was asking for more money than he needed. To line his pockets. This was not happening in a way that suggested blind adherence to some naive ideological nonsense.

It was about money, power, and control. That said, he now had a monetary target that he could use in planning and modeling going forward. Finally, this guy and the others like him around the world were thugs. Unmanageable. Eventually, they would have to be eliminated.

Yes, time was running out. Chicago, LA, Portland, Seattle. Even a few small cities were likely to follow suit. Typhon had primed them all, but now spontaneous combustion was spreading their destruction across the nation at an ever-increasing rate. His father was right again. The frog would soon jump out of the pot unless Typhon intervened. The mindless masses would soon awake and in their panic, mobilize in unpredictable ways, potentially complicating matters beyond their control.

CHAPTER THIRTEEN

BEST LAID PLANS

Singe, who was staring intently at one of the displays, blurted out suddenly, "guys, we got company!"

Mac rushed over. Black clad, armed men were leaping from two big choppers, their wheels only feet from the ground, and running towards the two ends of the residence. As they hit the ground, they tripped the inside perimeter motion detectors, and all hell broke loose. Blaring sirens erupted and high-powered perimeter floods popped on, illuminating the entire facility so brightly that some of the screens washed out momentarily.

Before Mac could alert Franklin, Curry came on the line. "Mac, what's going on?"

"We have ten-plus, maybe twenty armed men about to enter the building. Looks like they are taking up defensive positions across the grounds in front of the house. We might be able to get out through the back, but only if we hurry. If we don't finish this immediately, we'll have to lock ourselves inside, and I don't want to do that. Whatever happens, we need to finish the download."

Mac leaned on Carrie's console. "We're out of time. Are you in?" Mac asked.

"Yes, but I haven't located his financials. It's going to take more time than we have."

"Screw this," Singe interjected. "Let's just take the server and worry about the data later."

"Can we do that?" Mac asked.

"Actually, yeah. It's a good idea. It's right over there, about the size of a loaf of bread." She pointed to a rack against the wall. "I'm, shutting it all down."

"OK, good," replied Mac. "You have maybe a minute—we need to close the door. What can I do?"

"Stay out of the way," Swan shot back as she pushed out her chair and ran to the rack. Ten seconds later she pulled the server off its rails and handed it to Singe. "Put it in your backpack. And don't damage it."

"I won't," Singe replied wryly.

"Joe, Plan B. Leave LeMaster. Time to exfil," Mac instructed over his earpiece.

"We're on our way," came the reply.

They raced out of the entrance of the safe facility and Joe manhandled the big steel door shut as Curry fired a couple 45's into the sensors. No one was going to open the door from the outside. Mac and Singe led the way up to the main level and moved silently to the rear of the building. The team could hear the muffled voices and movements of several groups coming from areas in the front of the house.

The team met up in the main hallway, then ran together towards the main door. Suddenly, the corridor erupted with gunfire. They stopped and turned as one to see three of LeMaster's henchmen coming at them from around the left corner. Mac pulled off two quick silenced rounds, catching one man in the forehead and the second in the throat. The third got off a round before Singe nailed him in the chest followed immediately by a shot to the head.

Mac heard a grunt behind him and turned to see Franklin go down. Warsaw got to him first and began searching for the wound while checking his pulse with two fingers on his neck.

"I think he's OK," she said.

The ex-Seal's eyes fluttered open and for the second time that day. "Wa happen?"

"They got you in the vest," Mac responded. "Get him up, let's go."

"This is getting really old!" he exclaimed as they helped him to his feet.

Fifteen seconds later they were exiting out the back door. They took cover among the elaborate shrubbery and landscaping thirty yards behind and to the left of the house. In the distance, the thump-thump-thump of the Sikorskys echoed, the tail of one visible around the corner of the building.

Mac looked at Singe. "Can you fly one of those?"

Singe shot him a disapproving look. "What do you think?"

"OK. Let's move out then."

They skirted the edge of the compound, staying hidden in the shadows, and taking cover behind boulders and heavy cactus as they went. A few of LeMaster's reserves were positioned to cover the front yard, the rest had gone inside. As Mac's team reached a spot just fifteen yards from the chopper, five thugs came trotting around the far corner of the house. Curry and Warsaw already had their rifles trained on the area. Then, at least ten rounds of silenced NATO 556's hit their mark, their muted thuds unable to be heard over the rotor noise. Mac turned to see all five crumble. Then they rushed toward the chopper.

Singe snuck up behind the unsuspecting pilot and jabbed him in the shoulder with a hypodermic. The man slumped instantly, and Mac helped pull him out and onto the ground. Then Singe jumped into the pilot's seat as Mac helped Joe inside. Swan and Warsaw set up cover. Out of the corner of his eye Mac saw commandos pouring out of the front entrance and towards them.

Mac put on a headset, his earpiece still in place. "Let's go guys, things just got hot!"

By now they were squarely in the sights of several shooters with scoped rifles. With all inside, Singe lifted the chopper three feet off the ground, spun its nose around to face the shooters and throttled forward, full out. The enemy was now staring down a 7,000-pound, roaring machine accelerating toward them, blowing huge clouds of dirt and dust and impact just a second or two away. A few of them got off a shot or two but in the next instant they were all lying face down on the ground.

Fifteen minutes later Mac and his team were zooming along between two ridgelines, twenty miles out.

"Joe, you OK?" Mac asked.

"I'm good." He held up the mashed bullet between his forefinger and thumb, pried from his vest. "Just another souvenir," the big ex-Seal said with a grin.

Mac nodded to him and to each of his team in recognition. "That was tight. You guys were up to the task, though. It wasn't clean, and Clausen is going to be pissed about the collateral damage, but if that server has what we need, it was worth it. Remember, we are all protected. LeMaster will be highly motivated to get his data back, and depending on what's in there, we may have very significant leverage. By now he knows this was not your run-of-the-mill robbery; he may even suspect it was the government. In that case, he may decide to lay low for a while."

"If he doesn't decide to lay low," Warsaw added, "my gut tells me that he has a dozen contingencies and can be back in business and up and running without a hiccup in days or maybe even hours if left unimpeded."

A call over the radio interrupted their discussion. "Sikorsky Two, this is Sikorsky One, we have a proposition for you."

Mac, occupying the copilot's seat, shot a look at Singe. "Is there any chance they can catch us?"

Singe looked back, a worried look on his face. "Um, I suppose. We've been flying in the weeds to stay out of sight and off the radar. If they took off immediately after us and stayed high, though, yeah, they could have been following us the whole time. I could pop up and check the radar, but if they haven't found us yet, doing that would make it a certainty."

"OK, stay low then, and don't respond," Mac ordered. They remained silent. LeMaster repeated his entreaty, insistently this time. Obviously exasperated, LeMaster, his volume noticeably louder and no longer feigning cooperation, threatened, "I don't know who you guys are, but if you don't respond now, things will not end well for you. We have you in our sights."

"Mac..." Singe began worriedly as he pulled a circuit breaker on a side panel.

They were scanning the horizon and skies in all directions, looking for LeMaster.

"What?" Mac responded.

"I didn't think to turn off the transponder."

"What does that mean?" he asked.

"It means they probably know exactly where we are and have eyes on us right now. I just turned it off."

"Shit! Come on Peter, that seems like a rookie mistake." Mac exclaimed.

"What do you want to do?"

"Let me think for a minute."

Mac pondered the alternatives. LeMaster could see them, but they couldn't see LeMaster. Both birds had weapons. Until they changed something, LeMaster had the overwhelming advantage.

"Peter, can you turn around and see if they pop up on the radar? At least then we'll be on equal footing.

As a pilot, it was natural that Singe had always been intrigued with birds. Somewhat contrary to the image he portrayed, he was an avid birder. The Cooper Hawk, a somewhat smaller bird, scopes its prey from altitude and then retreats to a position out of sight. It stays low as it picks up velocity over small hills and then climbs, using rising terrain to camouflage its trajectory toward its meal. They never see the hawk coming.

"OK, I think I have an idea, actually. They are above us right now, but probably not too high—they will not want to be on the FAA's radar either. If we can get above and just behind them, they won't be able to see us. We'll have the advantage. Everyone should hold on to something."

Singe initiated his maneuver. Mac and the rest were pressed forcefully down in their seats as he turned suddenly down a curving ravine, rapidly descending to within feet of the treetops. He followed the ravine until they'd turned nearly 180 degrees, then turned sharply again up the side of a small mountain. Reaching the top, he used forward velocity to gain altitude. The Sikorsky's engine screamed as he used every bit of throttle, and they rose quickly. As their forward speed approached zero he began to rotate, still climbing. The horizon moved left to right as he searched for the other helicopter.

"There they are!" he yelled, pointing to the radar screen.

Sure enough, a green dot appeared on the display.

He scanned outside. "I have visual, dead ahead low."

Mac searched and after a second, he saw them. "It sounds risky, but I'm not sure we have a choice. I think LeMaster would rather take us out than let us escape with his server. What if we open the cabin door, fly right at them, and try to take them out? Maybe that will be enough to make them back off at least."

"I don't know if small arms will be enough to down them, but if we throw enough lead at them, it might just do the trick," Singe responded.

Mac nodded and looked backwards. "Lock and load, and open both side doors. And don't fall out, for God's sake."

"I'm approaching with our target below and on the right. And don't try to open the doors, that won't work—just slide the windows open," Singe cautioned. "Joe, you should aim at the engine and tail rotor. Carrie, you try to take out the pilot."

Singe completed the Cooper Hawk's run perfectly as they screamed down toward LeMaster, whose pilot had stopped in a hover after losing sight of them. Franklin and Swan rested their AR-15 barrels on the shelf of the right slide window.

And then they were on them. At fifty yards slightly behind and to their right, Mac could just make out an astonished face peering out the portside window of the passenger section. LeMaster. Franklin began to shower the upper section of the fuselage, moving from the tail rotor forward. Swan sighted in on the pilot's cabin and pulled off a series of rapid shots. It was difficult to tell if their shots were hitting home.

Mac could see activity now within the other bird, and what he saw next made his blood run cold. The left passenger door window was now open, and a large tube protruded, pointed at them. It was hard to tell if it was an RPG or a MANPAD with infrared guidance. If it was the latter, they were toast.

"I see it!" Singe yelled. "Hold on," and took them up fast and to the right.

Franklin and Swan fell to the cabin floor, then got up and repositioned quickly as their ascent stabilized.

"Sorry!" yelled Singe. They're on the left now, and they're speeding up. Guys, we must take them out immediately, or we'll have to run."

They were now above and to the right and just slightly behind LeMaster. Franklin started firing again at the tail rotor. Mac could see sparks and pock marks appearing on the tail and hull. Swan again sighted in and sprayed an entire clip into the windscreen, which instantly transformed into a massive white spider web. The safety glass was holding on for dear life.

The left-side window slid open as Swan released the empty magazine and reloaded, then showered the cockpit glass again. The entire windshield exploded inward as 150 miles per hour of airflow overcame its compromised integrity. Almost simultaneously, pieces of the tail rotor began to fly off and LeMaster's bird began to rotate out of control.

Singe yelled over the howling wind noise, "She's going down...oh shit!"

Mac felt as if everything were happening in slow motion. LeMaster's chopper was spinning as it fell. Singe followed it down at a safe distance and just above. Mac squinted. As the bird went round and round, he caught sight of LeMaster in the side window. Once, twice, three times in succession. It looked like he was smiling at them. The fourth time around, now close to the terrain, he now had the launcher pressed up against his cheek.

As the projectile cleared the tube, it didn't do much of anything, flung clear away from his team by the centrifugal force of the spinning helicopter. Singe had already broken off and gunned it to clear away. As they turned though, the missile's engine fired. It accelerated rapidly and began to turn in their direction. Singe was still taking them up and as good as he was, he had little chance evading a heat-seeking surface to air missile in a civilian luxury aircraft.

"Guys we have seconds before it hits," Singe yelled desperately.

"Head for LeMaster's bird *NOW*," Mac commanded.

Singe complied instantly. "I think I see where you're going with this."

The Sikorsky roared as Singe throttled to the max and drove it into a deep vertical dive. In no time they were on top of LeMaster's crippled coffin. The MANPAD had made another radical adjustment to it trajectory. As fast as it was it had small fins and made broad turns, but it was now on track towards them and closing fast.

"Peter," Mac yelled over the engine and wind noise, "you focus on the ground and LeMaster. I'll keep an eye on the missile. If it gets too close, I'll yell to pull up."

The world then accelerated from slow motion to hyper speed as Mac and his team witnessed LeMaster's S-76D impact the ground in an enormous explosion. Following closely, Singe pulled up hard and leveled off, flying right through the flames and billowing smoke. As they came out the other side, everyone held their breath and braced for impact. Almost immediately, a second explosion shook the aircraft violently. But they kept flying, and Singe began to climb. Circling around, they surveyed the crash site. The missile had obliterated LeMaster's chopper. The debris field was expansive, and fire engulfed the area.

Thirty minutes later, with their adrenaline finally receding, the team began to assess their situation. The mission had been successful. Jimmy LeMaster, the bane of free and fair social and mass media in America, was finally off the table. His files and data were in their custody, which would soon be exposed and exploited to help reverse an ever-present plague of corrosive fake news and unethical journalism. There was much more to do in this sector, but POTUS and the Agency had the high road and now, momentum.

Since they were ahead of schedule, they agreed to take the night off, get a good meal and some sleep. They'd head back to the east coast tomorrow. A date with Clausen was on the agenda for the following day to debrief and get updated. It would be the first time their entire team would meet with senior leadership, and they were anxious to prepare for Set Three.

CHAPTER FOURTEEN

INSIDE OUT

His first day back in Philly, Jefferey briefed his father on what he had learned in New York. Peter Gunderson was pleased with the additional insight and the deal he'd made, but also concerned about the accelerated pace of the insurrections and their spread. They had agreed to fund the first million but put conditions on the timing and distribution of the rest. They needed to keep a close watch on New York and how things evolved.

The next day, Jefferey flew to Washington, D.C. He wanted to get a handle on this elusive government ground force. It was time to cash in a favor. First stop, Georgetown. A fifteen-minute drive from downtown D.C., it was a quaint area and popular tourist attraction founded in 1751. A scenic six mile drive down the George Washington Pkwy, across Key Bridge and onto M Street and he was there. He parked a few blocks up on Wisconsin Avenue and walked casually down the sloping sidewalk, admiring the old Riggs Bank golden dome as it seemingly caught the entirety of the bright noon sun.

Cobblestone streets, high-end shops and restaurants adorned both sides of M street as it meandered adjacent to the grand Potomac River. His meeting was scheduled for 12:30 at Clyde's, an iconic watering hole. One of his favorite places in in the area, he'd reserved his favorite booth. As was his custom, he arrived ten minutes early and ordered a black coffee. Then he waited.

George Brewer joined the NSA twenty years ago, right out of George Washington University. He majored in mathematics with a minor in computer science, then slowly worked his way up the bureaucratic ladder. Now a senior manager, he was pulling down well over six figures and living comfortably in Laurel, Maryland, just a short drive from the Agency. While George had done well, he found himself stymied in his efforts to advance further. His superiors decided he wasn't senior leadership material and was passed over twice after making GS-15.

Brewer had always had an extravagant lifestyle. He owned a vacation house on Langford Bay, near Chestertown, Maryland with great fishing, crabbing, and access to the Chesapeake Bay. His teenage children loved the water. He built a sophisticated dock, with bubblers to protect it in the winter, and a boatlift. His Malibu M240 was next on the list, but he was in debt and bleeding red. His wife and kids were down there now, enjoying the spoils of his labors.

He was ambitious, but with his over-extended financial situation and his career at a dead end, he grew dissatisfied. After a chance meeting with an ex-state department retiree at a friend's cocktail party, he decided to pursue an opportunity that might just resolve both his career and financial woes.

He understood the risks involved. Snowden paid a steep price for his machinations. But unlike Snowden, he wasn't a whistleblower. He would cover his tracks. No one would ever find out. And so, after extraordinary precautions, he engaged in an arrangement with Jefferey Gunderson, an heir to a Philadelphia billionaire's future estate and an international financier in his own right.

After months of innocuous dialogue, Brewer and Gunderson hammered out an agreement. Brewer agreed to a retainer worth twice his annual Agency income, paid annually and deposited in an offshore, untraceable account. In return, he was to provide intelligence information to Gunderson on demand. After six months with no contact, he received the coded text scheduling today's meeting. As he entered the bar at precisely 12:30 pm, his trepidation had more to do with losing the income than what might be required of him. He was somewhat optimistic, figuring that termination of their agreement would not require a face-to-face meeting. In that, at least, he was correct.

Jefferey was careful about how many operational contacts he engaged with personally. In fact, it was rare. But with the most sensitive operators, he couldn't afford the risks inherent with using an intermediary. Krishinko ran point for overseas operations, but the U.S. government and intelligence agencies belonged to Jefferey. It had been a half year since he had seen Brewer. He'd grayed a bit at the temples.

As he entered, Brewer scanned the booths and nodded slightly when he saw Gunderson in the back of the room casually sipping his coffee.

"Good to see you again," said Gunderson, as Brewer took his seat on the opposite leather cushioned bench. "Would you like something to drink before we order?" he asked with a smile.

"Don't mind if I do. You know they make great Bloody Marys here."

They engaged in small talk as they ate. The crowd thinned and the booths emptied. Brewer finished his burger as Gunderson finished the last bite of his seared salmon. Gunderson paid the bill, and the two men got serious.

"Thanks for the lunch, Jefferey, but I imagine this luncheon is not just social," Brewer began.

"True," Gunderson replied. "I need some information for an investment opportunity. A multi-portfolio consortium I represent is concerned about some of its holdings in specific U.S. markets. A significant event occurred recently that resulted in a dramatic shift in the direction of this country's paradigm of education. My investors have become very nervous about this development and its impact on their strategies. We need to understand what is going on. Why it happened, and to prevent similar events from occurring. The rumors on the street are that this may have been coordinated. If true, we need to identify the players so our team can engage. You know, lobby and such. I can send you the details"

"I see," responded Brewer. "I can check with my sources. You're talking about what happened in Chicago, yes?"

"Yes. I need this turned around quickly or we may miss our window of opportunity."

"What's the timeline?" Brewer asked.

"Within twenty-four hours would be ideal, but no later than the day after tomorrow."

"That's aggressive," Brewer countered.

"That's the timeline, nonetheless," Gunderson shot back sternly. "Our arrangement exists so long as you can provide useful and timely information. In my business, old information is not information at all—it is historical data and no longer useful."

"Yes, I, I understand," stuttered Brewer.

Gunderson went on. "No emails, no phone calls. We have many competitors, and this topic is very sensitive, so use the dead drop." He rose curtly from the booth and strode out of the restaurant without a backward glance.

George Brewer let out a measured breath as he began to consider the implications of what he had to do. He'd heard rumblings in the building about sensitive activities driven by the director's office. And curious resource reallocations. It was a big agency, with thousands of employees and acres of facilities and his office was not involved in whatever it was, in any way. He felt a little nauseous now, realizing there may be more risk involved than he originally imagined.

There was something menacing about this guy Gunderson. Something dark. He couldn't put his finger on it. Brewer was beginning to understand that failure could have more serious consequences than losing out on substantial income.

Gunderson mentally reviewed their discussion as he drove toward the capital. He was satisfied he had set the right tone with Brewer. Veiled threats were much more effective with an asset like Brewer. Too much pressure and he could have a nervous breakdown, resulting in poor execution or exposure. If there really was an NSA operation formed against Typhon, he felt confident that Brewer would be able to confirm it. There was an outside chance that he could even identify the individuals involved, but he wasn't holding his breath. This was the reason his second meeting in an hour was so important.

On more than one occasion, unable to come through and fearing retribution, highly placed sources fed him fabricated information. Those assets were dealt with appropriately. Those outcomes were counterproductive, and often messy. So, Gunderson needed corroboration. Intel from inside the NSA, and from elsewhere.

Minutes later, he walked through the front door of Washington's oldest saloon, the Old Ebbit Grill on F Street, N.W. As he was seated, Jefferey eyed the blue placard gracing his table. The inscription read: *Many other famous statesmen, naval and military heroes, too numerous to mention here, have been guests of the house.*

Ironic, he thought. *It rings truer each time I sit here...*

Drumming his fingers as 3:00 pm came and went, he feigned patience. It was a virtue with which he was forced to abide, but one he found difficult to master. As 3:30 pm approached a booming voice and slap on the shoulder from behind made him jump.

"Hello Jefferey!" William Billings bellowed as he took his seat across from Jefferey. He was very influential—a longstanding member of the Senate Intelligence Committee and an old friend of his father.

"How are you, Senator?"

"Good as gold in a pot!" he replied with a grin. "Nice to see you again. Sorry I'm a bit tardy, but it's hard to break away when your staff is so needy. They're all so damn young and enthusiastic, it's enough to wear you out. I need a drink. Can I buy you one?"

Once the Senator was settled in, Jefferey cleared his throat to begin his pitch. He knew this conversation was going to be tricky. His had to be convincing and appear above board. His interests must come across as beneficial to Billings' platform and to traditional American values.

Before Jefferey could start, Billings asked, "Hey, how's your dad? I miss that old cuss."

"He's fine Senator, thank you for asking. He wanted to be here but couldn't make it—he sends his regards."

"No worries," he laughed. "It's probably a good thing. If he had come, we'd all be hammered before dinner."

Two decades earlier, Peter Gunderson strongly endorsed Billings' run for Senate and donated millions to his campaign. In the years that followed, he helped organize a Political Action Committee and several significant fund-raising efforts on behalf of his old friend. He never asked for anything in return. Of course, this was all part of Typhon's strategy.

Billings' comments were the perfect segue for Gunderson. "Kind of you to say so Senator. I know my father respects your service very highly and cherishes your friendship. He also values your advice. There is an issue he's been struggling with. He believes it is very important, and not just for him."

Billings leaned in, his interest piqued. "OK, well, what is it?"

"I guess it depends on your point of view. But in fairness, we wouldn't have bothered you if we didn't think it was worth your time. Let me preface my remarks by saying that some of this is speculation, and some is based on empirical evidence. I apologize in advance for being assumptive. As you know, my father has investments all over the world, and the vast majority of them here in the U.S. He is a true patriot—he believes in America and invests in that ideal. At the risk of sounding hyperbolic, there are things at play that are threatening his empire and by extension, the very bedrock of the American way of life."

Jefferey eyed the Senator. Confident he had his attention, he continued. "We have reason to believe that there is a deep-rooted and far-reaching conspiracy to shift control of our country in very fundamental ways. We believe it is being driven, not by international actors, but by U.S. citizens who feel disenfranchised by our core values and those of our constitution. The evidence is all around us. The rioting, the myriad special interest groups receiving unprecedented support and traction from invisible sources. We have mountains of data..."

His elbows on the table, Billings folded his swarthy hands and regarded Jefferey paternalistically. "I must admit, I don't like what I see going on in America right now, but socioeconomic and sociopolitical shifts are historically organic. They just happen, and we don't understand why or even really see they are happening until it's too late. Trying to reverse such a thing would take years and to be honest, the reversal always happens anyway, and it too happens organically. These ebbs and flows happen on a sine curve. It's the natural state of things—no one controls it."

"I agree," Jefferey nodded. "Historically. As you are aware, our investment group carefully monitors every aspect of American behavior. Our models are among the most accurate in the world and are based on societal trends, both micro and macro. In the last six months we have observed critical societal behaviors that have been aligning rapidly toward a common objective. The operative word being rapidly. What is happening now is an historical outlier—it does not jive with our modeling. The shift is developing much faster than it should if it were organic. And it is not a linear shift—it is accelerating. This means that there is an anomaly in the system. Something has been introduced. Something that has never existed before."

The Senator's eyes narrowed. "I have no doubt that your models are fantastic. I would say that there are things that have occurred in recent history that could have caused what you are seeing, however. The acceleration of computer technology, the advent of the age of instant communication and information. Social media. That's probably what your models couldn't predict, eh?"

"On the surface, I don't disagree Senator. These things must be programmed into a model retroactively, or as they are happening. Which would limit the accuracy. But our models are far more advanced than that. There is so much data, the algorithms are so state of the art, that they not only predict societal outcomes with a very high degree of certainty, *but they can also look out into the future and predict the anomalies.* The models then adjust predicted societal outcomes, even before the anomalies happen. That said, our models find that what is happening now is not mathematically plausible unless they are motivated by a common driver. The probability of it happening organically is less than one in a million."

The Senator raised his hands submissively. "OK, OK. Let's say all of that is true. I don't know anything about AI or predicting anomalies...but I can't even begin to imagine what person or organization could be running such a thing. I mean really, who in God's name would do that, and what would their end game be? They'd have to be well-funded, well-organized, and have incredible influence." He cocked his head and winked at Jefferey. "Like your dad's organization..."

Jefferey broke out in a wide grin.

The Senator continued. "I can't talk about anything classified of course, but I can tell you, in no uncertain terms, that the SIC is all over every American activist movement of any merit, including Antifa and BLM. We're watching some of the QAnon guys, but to be honest they're just a small group of disorganized misfits. But yeah, all of them. The NSA and Cyber Command monitor all the international bad actors—China, the Russians, North Korea, Iranians. We do see attempts, particularly from China, to influence and shape U.S. political, economic, and societal direction here in the U.S. It's a constant and evolving threat, but we do a pretty good job of staying on top of it. What we don't see, however, is any kind of united front. State actors operate on their own behalf. Sometimes their efforts cancel each other out. Why don't you tell me what your dad thinks is going on. Specifically."

"Yes, of course. In the last several weeks we've spoken with credible sources. They revealed to us that certain three-letter agencies set up compartmented operations to manage certain elements of widespread aberrant public behavior. The rioting, for example. By itself, that would not be news, except that our sources are telling us that instead of trying to investigate and arrest the perpetrators, they are possibly encouraging it. Maybe even funding it. While these assumptions are somewhat speculative, they are based on specific human intel and these sources are historically credible, so we have high confidence their reports are accurate."

The Senator was listening intently, his face becoming more incredulous with every word. "Certain agencies? You mean the FBI? DHS? You can't be serious?"

Jefferey sighed. "You're not going to like this, Senator. Our evidence points to the National Security Agency."

"You have got to be kidding me Jefferey," the Senator objected. "I know Jim Clausen personally and he is the last guy on the planet to be involved in anything like this. It's simply not possible!"

"I know it's hard to imagine or believe," Jefferey replied, "and I am certainly not implying the director is involved or even knows about it, just that it's happening. Someone, or more likely a faction within the NSA is involved. Bear in mind," Jefferey continued with emphasis, "that this is does not look like they are driven by a typical underlying disruptive ideology, like Marxism or Fascism. What they are doing doesn't fit. It appears to be a radical offshoot, one that evolved from a strong belief that our American Democratic Republic's founding principles have been twisted over time and are now failing."

"Your models told you all this?" Billings questioned, still incredulous.

"In a word, yes."

"But...that just doesn't compute. That's the opposite of what they would need to do. What you're telling me is, they are helping, or enabling erosion of the sanctity of our constitution."

Jefferey allowed himself the luxury of recalling his father's brilliance as he outlined the argument for the Billing's meeting. He'd said the key to convincing Billings is to tell him the truth, but with one small detail changed: change the protagonist. Demonstrate that NSA is the conspirator. Build evidence around that transposition that is solid enough to make it very believable, and therefore impossible for him not to act. Then show him a way to do it without risk. *With our help.*

Jefferey was ready for his response. "Senator, the only way to elicit radical change is with a significant emotional event. The larger the change, the more emotional and widespread the event must be. The group at the NSA is trying to incite the public to revolt against what is going on and to demand the government make sweeping changes, changes that will bring things back to normal, move things along that sine curve of yours."

Billings looked exhausted as he took it all in. Jefferey could see the wheels turning as he considered the bigger picture. He could almost hear what was going on in his head: *If this is even close to correct, I need to uncover it, stomp it out, immediately. For America. Could be beneficial to my political career as well. Committee Chair would be automatic. Maybe Senate Majority Leader. Maybe even higher...*

"Senator, we came to you for two reasons. One, we owe it to our investors to protect their assets. Two, and most importantly, my father and I believe very strongly in this country, its innate values and in the right to life, liberty, and pursuit of happiness of all its citizens. We have important and sensitive information that no one else has, and it is our duty to present it to someone of your character and ability who can quash this before things get out of hand."

"Jefferey, this is a serious allegation, as serious as it gets. You have my attention. I have some ideas about how to investigate this without causing too much of a stir, but what is it exactly you think you need from me?"

Jefferey saw what the Senator was doing. He wanted the senior Gunderson's opinion on what to do. The trap had been laid, and Billings walked right into it. Jefferey offered him the hard evidence he would need to expose the entire scheme and added that a leak to the New York Times would help move things along quickly. Serious wrongdoings within the government tended to stay internal and are oftentimes never prosecuted—the American people deserved to know. Billings should have sole authority on how to handle the inquiry and subsequent judicial action.

Billings liked the plan and committed to launch an investigation of the NSA's activities using SIC assets already assigned to the Agency. He agreed to start the following morning and estimated he could have at least some preliminary findings within forty-eight hours. They shook hands and departed, each with high expectations for what was to come.

Jefferey mused as he gazed out on the glowing lights of the U.S. Capitol from his first-class cabin window. *Today was a good day.* He was becoming more optimistic about navigating the high-stakes operations his father entrusted him with. In fact, his confidence was growing that Typhon's plan and its execution were likely back in the category of *unstoppable.*

He'd stay in town for now, at least until George Brewer and Billings reported back. He really got off on this type of field work and had prepared for it with years of training that began even before he went off to college. Self-defense and martial arts, weapons, and marksmanship. Survival and recon training with foreign Typhon partners consumed his summers. Finally, a grueling and dangerous series of real-world assassinations teamed with an elite para-military team in the Far East against legitimate ISIS targets. That three-month stint cost his father a cool $250,000. There were times when his life was, without a doubt, on the line, but that experience changed everything for him. He knew, *really knew*, how to kill and not be killed. Something so few have ever mastered. On that thought and with a satisfied smile, he switched off the overhead light for a short nap before landing in Philly.

CHAPTER FIFTEEN

NICHOLI

It had been a whirlwind trip so far, made almost tolerable while wrapped in the luxurious comfort of Typhon's Gulfstream G650ER private jet. With an 8,000-mile range and cruising speed of Mach 0.9, Krishinko was able to reach all his destinations quickly, and without connections.

His first stop was London. Historically, Typhon's Commissar of the European Union had covered the UK. However, the Kingdom withdrew from the EU in 2020, and a new representative was appointed. That was a challenge to make happen. Despite Brexit, Gunderson was tempted to keep the old organizational structure in place, but their EU Commissar, Wart Von Stemp convinced him otherwise. The UK's socioeconomic situation was in a downward trend, in part due to unchecked immigration within a system that could not keep up. This dynamic helped Typhon's objective of societal disruption; the associated religious movements and backlash were inherently problematic. Authoritarian models such as Marxism dealt with it quite well. The CCP essentially mandated that the state itself was the national faith to avoid this dilemma specifically. In the end, Von Stemp had argued there was simply too much going on in the UK for him to deal with it while shouldering the rest of the EU. Which left Krishinko with the challenge of sourcing a new Commissar.

Six months earlier, a candidate surfaced from an unlikely source. Her name was Jasmine Snow, a career MI-6 officer working at the Secret Intelligence Service's Vauxhall Cross headquarters. Snow joined the service a decade earlier and was a solid analyst who wanted nothing more than to be a field operative. She envied her peers whose assignments took them all over the country. Eventually, after repeated requests, she got her wish and was assigned to first level field operations. It turns out she was quite good at her new role and went on to receive more and more complex assignments.

Snow was easy to look at. A fitness nut, she was slender yet proportionately muscled. Straight ebony hair, high cheekbones, and fierce hazel eyes. An intense personality combined with a disarming sense of humor to complete the rare package. Adversaries were often at a disadvantage from the get-go, caught up in her allure and unaware of her physical prowess.

One fateful day while investigating an international drug ring, she discovered that a corrupt London detective, working undercover, was colluding with the drug smugglers to grease the rails for their logistics efforts. She passed the evidence to his superiors. Sometime later, the evidence disappeared from the police evidence locker, and the case was dismissed. If that had been all that happened, it would have been unfortunate. However, the entire operation was being monitored several levels above her pay grade. Unseen political forces were major stakeholders in the various possible outcomes of the operation. Unbelievably, she ended up discredited and was demoted for failure in the field. A fall gal.

She fought the result and lost decisively. Then and there, Jasmine Snow decided the system was rigged. If she were ever presented with an opportunity, she would get even. Her career and dreams were shot, her life essentially in ruins. And there was nothing she could do about it because she was just a pawn in a game riven with corruption.

But she still needed a purpose in life and a team she could work with. People she could trust with a mission that wasn't buried beneath layers of bureaucracy and masqueraded as something that it wasn't. She had to be clear about what impact her work would have on the world. Krishinko had been watching her for some time and set out to persuade her that Typhon was the answer. Snow was already convinced that the world needed fixing and joining with Typhon promised a purer approach to society's ills. So, she signed up. Enthusiastically.

The two met for two hours at a back-alley pub in central London, where Snow shared her view that with the proper resources and incentives, it would be possible to turn, tap into, amplify, and promote secular inequities and perceived social biases and racism to fuel disruptions to elicit the radical change Typhon was seeking. Krishinko listened intently. He was intrigued but remained skeptical.

"What if it's not enough? What would you do then?" he asked.

Snow's answer was measured, but unexpectedly bold. "If it fails, the next step would be to remove the playmakers. Without key leadership in place on both sides of a confrontation, the people take over. Mob rule would ensue with confrontations along financial class, religious, and ethnic lines. General anarchy. This would be the key moment when Typhon should move into the governance vacuum," she explained.

Krishinko was impressed. Her ideas, though radical, might yet be necessary. These measures in the UK might even serve as a beta test for other countries where Muslim and other ethnic minority mass migrations were literally destroying the very fabric of the indigenous culture.

As Krishinko prepared to conclude their meeting, he asked one final question of his new UK Commissar. "I know you are not yet aware of what your contingency plan is. If I bring you on board, you'll be briefed on it straight away. But for me to do that, you must agree to it, sight unseen. Failure to do so would result in very swift, and very permanent measures that make what happened to you at MI-6 pale in comparison. But at least with Typhon, you have clarity and understand exactly what will happen if you fail. So…Jasmine, if we determine that your contingency is required, are you prepared and willing to carry it out, immediately and without hesitation?"

"Nicholi, Britain is being overrun by Muslims and other non-citizens because of pre-Brexit EU open borders policies. I may be jaundiced about the corruption in our government, but I love my country, deeply. I have a broad list of contacts and good relationships with law enforcement and influential conservatives who are passionate about taking our country back. When the time comes, they will rally around me and the cause, and do whatever is necessary to save The UK and its heritage. The answer to your question is a resounding *yes*."

Krishinko departed London Luton Airport. The Gulfstream reached cruising altitude and almost immediately, it began its descent into Paris Le Bourget. After landing, Krishinko was met by a Rolls Royce and driven directly to his favorite place to stay, Hôtel Particulier Montmartre. Off the beaten path, the enchanted hotel was hidden down an old-world alley in the fabled artist quarter of Montmartre. The superb cuisine and attentive service, not to mention isolation from the frenetic bustle of tourism ever present in the City of Love made Particulier his favorite hotel in all of France, if not Europe. He would rendezvous this evening with Wart Von Stemp.

The EU represented twenty-seven member nations and over 450 million souls, making its population roughly fifty percent larger than the U.S. With open borders between countries and a common currency, it was commonly viewed as a quasi-U.S. model. But that is where the similarities ended. Relatively recent, holistic governance had little effect upon thousands of years of strong, regionalized cultural and linguistic identities. In fact, there was a kind of societal schizophrenia that characterized the love-hate relationship between its members, and Brussels had done nothing of significance for the whole that was not seen as a constant irritant to its individual members. There was non-stop bickering on every policy. Overreach of authoritative control had stifled nearly all meaningful advancement of common or regional goals and calcified its effectiveness. And because of its traditionally inbred leadership, the EU rarely saw leaders emerge from outside its elite class. It was a perfect target for Typhon—a bureaucratic quagmire rife with incompetence, and just waiting for re-birth into a new order.

Wart Von Stemp trotted up the ancient steps until he saw number 23. Other than the number, it was an unmarked gate to the entrance of the 19th century mansion. He pushed a button to the side and heard a faint buzzing nearby. A smartly dressed bellhop opened the gate, took his bag, and showed him to the suite. Krishinko had already arrived and greeted him at the door. They exchanged a warm embrace and went inside.

The two had known each other for decades and had been through some hair-raising experiences together. Von Stemp was of German descent with a royal lineage. His family barely escaped Hitler's wrath, fleeing first to France and then to Bulgaria. They survived the war but lost everything. Von Stemp's grandfather returned to Germany in 1947 and was able to recover some of the family's assets, but it was never the same. In the late 1950's, his father moved the family to Brussels to take a position with the newly formed European Economic Community (EEC), which evolved later into the European Union.

After college, Von Stemp followed his father's lead and procured a position in the EU. He steadily moved up the ranks and was well respected by his colleagues. His primary responsibilities focused on strategic planning and EU member relations. For Von Stemp, it was the perfect job. He remained unmarried, allowing him unchecked freedom to engage in his passions. And he had a few. When he wasn't skiing or riding horses, boxing and martial arts filled his free time. His social and relationship skills were flexibly refined—he was just as comfortable chugging a pint of ale with a group of swarthy friends as he was eloquently toasting the person of honor at a ritzy charity gala.

He was tall and muscled, even in middle age. Thick, straight blond hair and angular Teutonic features made him appear younger than his forty-three years. Natural good looks and a raucous sense of humor made him a ladies' favorite—and Von Stemp enjoyed the ladies. All in all, Von Stemp's experiences and career had had been good thus far. But it hadn't quite lived up to his family's heritage and legacy.

That huge, unwieldy organizations could effectively govern was foreign to his thinking. After twenty years of studying the EU, he'd come to believe it was an incontrovertible truth—a truth he shared with Nicholi Krishinko. His chance meeting with Krishinko at an EU conference fifteen years ago began as a friendship, eventually evolving into much more than that. Their backgrounds were similar, and they shared many beliefs beyond politics and governance.

Krishinko emerged from the failed communism of the USSR in much the same way that Von Stemp's family escaped the horrors of Nazi fascism. For both, their perspective was that Russians and Germans were proud people with storied histories, and that their modern governments were both disasters by comparison. It was inevitable Krishinko would recruit Von Stemp to the Typhon management team. He was well positioned in the ruling EU structure and his credentials dovetailed perfectly with Typhon's leadership profile requirements.

They sat comfortably on the plush high-backed chairs, separated by an 18th century coffee table. Its dark polished mahogany reflected the soft yellow light of the crystal chandelier above. Krishinko started the conversation with a question about the state of disruptions across the EU.

Von Stemp gave him a country-by-country overview. "For some time now, the members have been dealing with a serious immigration issue. While migrants have come from everywhere, Africa, the middle east, even Asia, a high percentage are Muslim and bring their ideology with them. As you know, Sharia law does not permit integration or moderation, so that population is a real problem."

"Yes," responded Krishinko to his friend, "it's particularly bad in the UK."

"That said," Von Stemp continued, "there are other problems precipitating across the continent. The Yellow Jackets here in France, for example. They are an organized, radical economic movement focused on eliminating income disparity and forcing equity measures into labor practices. To add fuel to the fire, we are experiencing an extraordinary increase in imported domestic terrorism. Constructs. Various facsimiles of Antifa, and even BLM."

"That is good to hear. I'm glad you referred to them as constructs," commented Krishinko, "since we literally designed them. It still amazes me that Typhon's strategy of identity segmentation has been so effective. We knew we would sow tremendous dissent, but never did we imagine how creative these power groups could be, or that they could get away so successfully with attempts to camouflage a political agenda with societal inequity. Is it working?"

"Not really, most mainland Europeans don't really buy into racial or social inequity. Particularly the Germans. Equality, yes. Equity, no.

That said, we have our fair share of screaming liberals and a naive younger generation who coopt these constructs for their own insidious purposes, or so they can feel like they belong to something greater than themselves. So they can say they have a purpose in life."

"What about the governments? How are they responding, and what is their plan?" asked Krishinko.

Von Stemp chuckled. "They are clueless. They don't understand what is driving the disruptions, let alone how to deal with them. Deer in the headlights."

"Wart, are we in control of this immigration issue? Or has it gotten away from us?"

"We are not in control yet," Von Stemp replied. "We may need to shift our focus to individual countries, to divide and conquer. It's additional work but will be more effective in the long run."

"OK." Krishinko replied. "Send me the details and I'll run it by the team. We need to make sure that any late adjustments will align globally. I'll give you feedback and directions a day or two after I get home."

"Understood," replied Von Stemp.

"One final question," Krishinko added. "Have you seen or heard anything about a U.S. government effort, probably three-letter, trying to undo our work by reversing disruptions, slowing things down, diverting activities, that kind of thing?"

Von Stemp took a moment to respond. "I don't think I've seen anything that I can't explain."

"Ok," responded Krishinko, "let's call it a night and go have a little fun for old times' sake."

Krishinko was up early the next morning. He had some serious thinking to do—including in preparation for a follow-up call to Jefferey. At 10:00 am he packed up, said au revoir to his hotel friends and made his way back to the airport. He was served lunch on board the Gulfstream as he finalized his report. He needed to be on a video call by 3:00 pm Paris time, 9:00 am in Philadelphia. A twenty-seven-inch flat panel jumped to life as the trans-oceanic video connection linked up. The encrypted picture flickered for a second, then a life-sized image of Jefferey Gunderson appeared.

"Hey Jeff, good morning," Krishinko began.

"And good afternoon to you Nicholi. How is the trip going?"

"Actually, things are going well. Snow and Von Stemp seem to be on top of it; both gave me a solid overview of our progress, as well as the challenges facing them and their areas of responsibility. More importantly, they have rational and well thought out recommendations on how we should continue."

"That's good to hear, Nicholi," said Gunderson. "Sum it up for me."

"The majority of our disruptions are growing and gaining traction. The biggest issue is related to radical Islamic extremists migrating into the UK, the EU countries, and other regions. I know we considered these factors, but their movements have metastasized more rapidly than we anticipated."

"Interesting. Fortunately, we don't have that problem in the U.S. yet," commented Jefferey. "So, our problem here is controlling the *pace* of disruptive escalations, and internationally it is managing and controlling disruptions so that they remain in line with our strategies."

"Yes. But I'm worried, Jeff, that we don't have a synchronized approach to dealing with these problems. In the UK, we need to marginalize opposition leadership. In the EU, we'll need a more surgical approach within individual countries. In the U.S., we either need to slow the disruptions, or to pull the trigger—overt engagement. It's getting a little more complicated than we foresaw. Messy, even. We might think about developing a strategy that will universally resolve all these complications."

Gunderson chuckled. "That's a tall order, Nicholi. What's your idea?"

"First," replied Krishinko, "I think we need to circle the wagons. As you know, I was about to fly to Tehran to meet with Yakim Abdul, our Iran-based Mid-East Typhon Commissar, and then meet with Suela Chenzi in Hong Kong. Now I believe I should return to headquarters for an emergency strategy meeting with you and your father to figure this out. I can videoconference with Abdul and Chenzi on the flight back. I'll still have their status reports, and I can bring them to the meeting."

Gunderson had a lot on his plate, but he felt Krishinko was right. Things were unraveling in the field, and they needed to adjust, or the proverbial shit was likely to hit the fan.

"Ok, Nicholi, scrap the backend of your trip and get back here. I'll speak with Dad and set it up."

144

"Ok, Nicholi, scrap the backend of your trip and get back here. I'll speak with Dad and set it up."

CHAPTER SIXTEEN

SET THREE

The Apogee Team set down on the tarmac at Andrews Air Force Base. They'd decided to fly LeMaster's Sikorsky back to DC and into custody of the Agency. They needed to scrub it for intel, and they also wanted to have a hand in managing the outcome of the forthcoming FAA investigation of the crash. The trip back gobbled up twelve hours, with the refueling stops at military bases along the way. They used the extra time to refine their final brief for the Admiral, scheduled for 8:00 am the next morning.

At 7:00 AM, a black Suburban with dark tinted windows parked in front of the hotel lobby entrance and they piled in. Next stop, the Building. They arrived about an hour later. After clearing security, the team was directed through a maze of corridors to the lobby of the Director's Executive Suite on the 9th floor.

"Mr. Sisco, very good to see you again," said Martin Stabler, Executive Assistant to Admiral Clausen. He rose to shake Mac's hand. He turned to greet the rest. "Welcome to you all. The Admiral is just finishing up another meeting. If you will follow me into the conference room, we have coffee and bottled water if you like."

They followed him through the side door into the room. Moments later, one of the large wooden panels on the opposite wall opened and

Admiral Clausen walked through, a mug of coffee in one hand and a thick binder in another.

As he entered, he turned back while closing the panel and spoke,

"Thank you all for coming," he began. "I want to begin by thanking you all for agreeing to take on this dangerous assignment, and again for the apparent success you've had thus far." He smiled warmly. "I'm looking forward to hearing all the details."

Each of the team knew the Admiral to one degree or another, and some had worked for him in various capacities. They all respected and trusted him, which had a great deal to do with why they were all there in the room at that moment. Clausen then went around the room, visited casually with each member of the team, and personally thanked them again. Clausen then called the meeting to order.

"First," he began, "I want each of you to know the President sends his appreciation for your service in this operation. He also wanted me to make it clear that he has your back."

Mac glanced around the table and could see and feel the positive vibes this comment elicited. It was more than reassuring. So many of these assignments were unsanctioned, which sometimes left agents naked against potential blowback.

"Now," the Admiral continued, "As you know, Apogee is a Top-Secret FACET initiative. As such any leaks must be avoided at all costs. That said, even with all the Agency's security protocols, shit happens, so be forewarned."

He stopped as Martin entered and handed each of the team a leather binder with a red seal on the top left.

"Thank you, Martin," Clausen said as his aide closed the door silently behind him. "I have allocated two hours for this briefing but have cleared my calendar for the rest of the day, in the event we need more time. Any questions before we begin?" The room was silent.

"OK then. Let's begin with an overview of Sets One and Two. Please don't leave out any details, no matter how insignificant they may seem. This meeting is being recorded, by the way, in case we need to revisit anything for insight or clarification. Also, there is no such thing as a dumb question, so ask away, you can be sure I will. Take it away, Mac."

Mac pulled out his briefing notes, cleared his throat and began. Over the next forty-five minutes the dialogue was robust. Each member of the team participated, filling in blanks, adding nuance. The result was a vivid picture of both operations. Clausen listened intently, interrupting at times with questions.

As they concluded, Clausen stood up from his chair. "Let's take a fifteen-minute break, recharge our coffee and move to agenda item two, which is what the big 'M' has been doing."

Back from the break, Clausen began again. "Now for the top-level activities. My brief won't be as detailed as yours. A lot of what I've been managing is driven by secondary and tertiary actors. Additionally, plausible deniability is never a bad thing and *need to know* at this level is in place for everyone's protection. I might add that without this level of assurance, none of our advocates would even come to the table."

Mac and his team were stunned by the global scope of Apogee and the degree to which the President, the NSC, and the NSA were involved. Clausen informed them of a series of conversations between the President and select world leaders. These meetings were conducted on the 'red screen,' a VTC equivalent of the red phone in the oval office. The President initiated those calls shortly after Mac had his initial meeting with Clausen, just two weeks ago. The plan he and the NSC hatched was bolstered by an international coalition with America's closest allies, and with specific other countries experiencing serious disruptions.

The calls received surprisingly positive responses. When one's homeland is threatened, political differences took a back seat. The concept that 'the enemy of my enemy is my friend' rang true as unrest spread across the globe. His first calls went to the Five Eyes members: Australia, Canada, New Zealand, and the United Kingdom. These nations already had an intelligence sharing arrangement with the U.S., but not to the extent suggested for this effort. With the help of Clausen and his team, President Holbrook and the NSC organized the coalition by establishing a set of broad operational principles that would bind them in executing a closely coordinated global solution.

Each country would execute its own operations while abiding by mutually beneficial guidelines while keeping the rest of the coalition members informed. Their greatest challenge would be mitigating public awareness. Leaks were inevitable, so they developed a comprehensive media plan to shape public opinion, discredit allegations and fake news, and to avoid panic. The irony that their plan more or less amounted to fighting the truth with their own fake news, while uncomfortable, was nevertheless endorsed by all and justified by the philosophy that the end more than justified the means.

Holbrook's most difficult calls were to allies in the Middle East. Though U.S. and mid-east relations were favorable and had continued to improve since his election, the Arab nations had to be handled in a more delicate manner. In the end, however, concerns about radical Islamic terrorism and Iran's overt threats were enough to bring them into the fold. The Saudi King, who was especially fond of acronyms, coined the name of the coalition: NATCOG. It stood for the Nationalist Coalition Group, a name that reinforced the autonomy and independence of each member country.

Hungary, Poland, and Czechoslovakia were all-in, and several others followed. But President Holbrook was forced to tread lightly with Western Europe. He approached each country individually, bypassing the EU. He knew that as soon as he engaged any but his most stolid European friends, the EU would hear about it, so he arranged his calls back-to-back and made his pitch to the majority of EU members in a single day.

Clausen paused and leaned back in his chair and took a sip of his (now cold) coffee. "Before I go on, any questions?"

Pat Curry raised his hand. "Sir, were there any naysayers? Did you run into resistance with any particular countries?"

"The result has been largely positive," Clausen answered. "France and Germany were concerned about potential blowback from countries that were not included in the coalition, like China and Russia. So, they are still mulling their positions and the EU is consulting its members before taking a final decision, which we anticipate by the end of the week."

"What happens if they don't sign up?" asked Gunderson.

The Admiral nodded. "We knew certain European countries would be the toughest sell, so the President went after the low hanging fruit first. By the time he got to the troublemakers, he already had over 40 countries committed. It's just a matter of time, to be honest."

"Admiral, what do you think happens when China, Iran, Russia and the North Koreans get wind of NATCOG?" Mac asked.

Clausen's face darkened. "We have a pretty good idea how they may respond. The Chinese will complain loudly, engage in provocations, perhaps impose new trade restrictions. No real news there. The Russians will do what they always do—deny they have any problems internally and squelch any uprisings while trying to discredit the U.S. Also predictable. North Korea may shoot off a couple more missiles to nowhere but will otherwise lay low unless they see some opportunity to benefit from the chaos. They will also never admit they have a problem. Iran, while predictable in their rhetoric, are so unstable at this point, and their economy is so weak from our sanctions that they could use the turmoil to make a desperate move of some kind. We are keeping our ear to the ground. With these authoritarian regimes, this global conspiracy is not necessarily perceived by them as relevant. They control their people with fear, a tactic that is, to a point, effective in preventing an uprising, so they see it as much less of a risk. But let me emphasize *to a point.*"

Clausen continued. "The National Security Council is handling the operational aspects of NATCOG. The Secretary of State is managing country members via their Ambassadors in D.C., and SECDEF and the Chairman of the Joint Chiefs are working directly with their foreign counterparts. Once the President gave us the go ahead, we engaged the rest of The Principals Committee, which includes the Cabinet-level senior interagency forum. It is convened and chaired by the National Security Advisor. Regular attendees include the Secretary of State, the Secretary of the Treasury, the Secretary of Defense, the Attorney General, the Secretary of Energy, the Secretary of Homeland Security, the White House Chief of Staff, the DNI, the Chairman of the Joint Chiefs of Staff, the Director of the CIA, the Homeland Security Advisor, and the Ambassador to the UN."

"OK," Swan interrupted, "that is a big group. How can you possibly hope to keep this out of the press? My guess is the New York Times will have all the details within a week."

"Great question, Carrie," said the Admiral. "Obviously, it's not going to be easy, but special care has been taken to maintain the outward impression of business as usual. POTUS won't be changing his routine, nor will the other members of the NSC. All NATCOG meetings will be held outside normal duty hours and via secure methods. Recordings of those meetings are distributed daily to Principal members and are eyes-only FACET restricted. All participants have been informed that any leaks are to be considered treason and will be adjudicated swiftly as such."

"Well," Mac intoned, "I sure hope that works. It hasn't before. At least, not lately."

"For the sake of this country, I hope so too," Clausen responded seriously as he closed his binder.

After another short break, the Director continued. "Ok folks," he began, "we're on the last lap. This part of our agenda is all about dialogue, feedback, and brainstorming. We need to refine your upcoming Ops Sets and align them with our strategic initiatives. There will be situations where your assignments are predicated upon our results, and vice versa. In my experience, the best-laid plans are flexible to the point of, well, not being much of a plan at all. In other words, we will have to go with the flow. Collect, analyze, and understand the right intelligence and respond appropriately to win the game. Does everyone understand?" Clausen asked hopefully.

Almost in unison, the team responded, "Yes sir!"

"Good," Clausen smiled appreciatively. "The reasons each of you were chosen were not just because you were the best at what you do, or that you can think on your feet better than anyone else, but because of your collective capabilities as a team. That, with some of the most powerful elements of the U.S. government behind you will win the day.

"Now, let's talk Sets. We've defined a series of tactical operations, like the two you've already completed. I must warn you though—they are going to be significantly more challenging."

"Why is that, Admiral?" Mac jumped in. "I would argue that Set Two was pretty challenging." The team members looked at each other, nodding in agreement.

"There are several reasons, Mac, but most importantly, you will be operating on foreign soil. In some cases, your team will be split up to execute strikes in parallel, which depletes your strength and increases the risk of exposure. More things could go wrong. It's not ideal, but our models predict a higher probability of success doing it this way. Additionally, and not to sound pessimistic, but it provides redundancy in the event an op fails. If half the team is compromised, we still have half a team.

"Set 3 is pivotal because it targets the fuel of the fire. Money. Taking away their finances is like taking oxygen out of the air. The movement dies. This set has several legs to it. The funding for these disruptions comes from various places around the world, so you will be travelling quite a bit.

"The Secretary of the Treasury is leading the NSC action on this set, with NSA support. We've identified several global investment firms with U.S. ties that have been under scrutiny for some time. Treasury is going to conduct a surprise audit on each of them, beginning tomorrow. We will try to stress their management and hopefully, shake loose some leads that point to the bad actors. We will also put a squeeze on their money flow. Some of you will be following up on treasury's scare tactics, undercover of course, to see what you can dig up. Our objectives are to ID any firms that are funding disruptions and to tie them back to the people pulling the strings."

"And how are we going to do that, specifically?" Mac interjected.

"Mac, when we collaborated with you and your father on building the Apogee team, we were very particular about the skill sets. This is the point where these choices become so critical. We need to send two of you to New York to dig into these company's finances. Our federal audit team will provide you with server information, passwords, and whatever help you need to bypass their digital security layers."

"Gee, I wonder who might be on that team," Swan said, smiling broadly as she glanced at Curry.

The big Aussie smiled back. "This should be a ruddy walkabout."

Clausen went on, "Yes, Carrie and Pat, you two will carry that mission out. You'll have to work with my office to coordinate with Treasury. Be back here at 8:00 am tomorrow to be briefed on your covers and to receive your credentials. You'll head to New York in the afternoon.

"Now, the next leg of this four-legged stool is closely connected to the New York op," the Admiral continued. "Signals intelligence tells us the most likely repository for much of their funding is in the Cayman Islands and Swiss banks. Luckily for us, there is a one-week international banking conference on Grand Cayman Island that begins later this week. One of the agenda items is focused on the cultural and societal impacts of global banking. We've already registered you, Elaine, to present. We also managed to get Peter invited to lead a panel discussion on the impact of legal disparities in international lending. We even built you a PowerPoint brief, but I suspect you will want to improve upon our rudimentary efforts.

"You will travel as colleagues so you can interact together freely without drawing attention. There are several social events on the agenda that will provide an opportunity for you to interact with other attendees. We've pulled together some rather embarrassing information on a handful of key bank executives from both the island and several Swiss banks. Your assignment is to use this information as leverage to extract intelligence on their activities related to NATCOG funding, and to find out where the money comes from. Any questions?"

"Will there be any beach time?" quipped Elaine.

Clausen smiled. "If you can combine work with play, sometimes that's the most effective way to do these things. Now, let's get to the next op. Information our analysts gleaned from LeMaster's server includes a trove of actionable intelligence that will help us, and the FCC illuminate certain illegal practices being employed by mainstream media. There will be some high-level indictments, and on a broader scale, certain outlets may be stripped of their journalistic designation, unless major changes are made. And some web-based companies are going to lose Title 47 Section 230 protection.

"We were also able to break into a folder containing very curious data. On some of the data, LeMaster used a somewhat archaic, but effective encryption scheme called a 'onetime pad,' which uses a key from a reference document that only the sender and receiver know. If you don't have the key, there is no way to access the file. Decryption algorithms are useless against it. Some of the data was less secure, however, and we unearthed lists of names, addresses, dates of meetings, and a slew of text messages.

"When we analyze content like this—emails, texts, what have you, we look for repeated words, numbers, and phrases. If it is repeated, it usually has more value. One word repeated numerous times was Typhon. In Greek mythology, Typhon was the father of all monsters and had one hundred heads. It's likely that Typhon is the name of the enemy organization, or the code name for the person or persons in charge. Mac and Joe, one of my analysts is going to give you all the relevant files. Follow up and try to get us some answers."

Mac leaned forward. "Admiral, have you identified anyone on the lists of names you think might be part of the…*Typhon*…upper echelon?"

"Yes," the Admiral responded positively. "There are two we are pretty sure about, and given how unique the names are, we were able to track them down. Nicholi Krishinko and Wart Von Stemp. We traced Krishinko to Munich, Germany. Von Stemp lives in Paris, France."

CHAPTER SEVENTEEN

TAKEDOWN

Peter Gunderson lounged in a kitchen chair at the Mainline mansion, gingerly sipping from a mug of hot coffee. He was waiting on Jefferey, who was likely dodging commuter traffic on Lancaster Pike at this time of day. Things had been on an upswing recently, capped by his son's briefing on the success of his Washington, D.C. trip. But today, things took an unexpected turn. James LeMaster's perished in a helicopter accident in the Sierra Blanco Mountains of New Mexico this morning. It was all over the news.

Gunderson never met LeMaster, despite the fact he was one of Typhon's key influencers. To meet him would have meant breaking the chain of anonymity. He was aware LeMaster had engaged with both Krishinko and Von Stemp. The global media reach and influence LeMaster controlled required continuous engagement that simply could not be left to underlings. Besides, LeMaster was so arrogant and demanding that no other arrangement would have been practical. Gunderson had ultimately agreed that the risk of having LeMaster engage directly with his core team was worth the reward, but now he was not so sure.

He heard footsteps approaching and Jefferey appeared in the doorway.

"Good morning son," Gunderson greeted him. "Get some coffee, I am anxious to hear more about your meetings in Washington."

Jefferey acknowledged him and wasted no time filling a cup. "Have you seen the news today?"

"Yes," his father replied. "I hope we don't have a problem."

"Perhaps, perhaps not," replied Jefferey. "There's no such thing as a coincidence."

"What do you know about it?" the older man asked.

Classic Peter Gunderson. It was barely 8:00 am, the news had just hit the wire and the old man was expecting answers. There was a time when this would have irritated him, but he eventually learned that his father's relentless drive and unapologetic demands for results was a strength, a true game changer in a world of mediocrity.

"I made some calls on the way over," he answered. "As you know, I had an undercover guard placed within his team in Ruidoso, but it still took some time to get good feedback. Bottom line, his death was no accident. There was an attack on his residence two nights ago. Our guard initially figured it was a professional robbery attempt. They breached perimeter security, overcame the guards, and locked them all in a utility room while they ransacked the house. LeMaster evaded them and with four of his personal bodyguards, he reached his safe room in the basement, which is virtually impregnable. He then got on the horn and called in reinforcements from his security headquarters in El Paso. The attackers were able to gain entrance to the safe room, however. El Paso scrambled a tactical unit with two Sikorskys and flew to the complex. Just as they were entering the facility, there was a firefight. The intruders escaped, by highjacking one of the choppers. They killed several guards on the way out. LeMaster pursued in the second Sikorsky. I can only assume that he engaged them. Our inside guy was not on the second bird, and is being questioned by the local authorities, the FAA, and the FBI. He is sticking to his story of a failed robbery attempt. He knew nothing about the crash, which was discovered and called in by a couple of hikers who were camping out on an adjacent ridge and saw the smoke."

Peter Gunderson had listened intently to his son's report without any interruptions. He was silent a long time as he pondered his son's account. "Any word on the whereabouts of the other Sikorsky?"

"Not yet, but I'm looking into it. They would've had to touch down within a 500-mile radius for refueling and we are checking every airport within that range."

Just then, Jefferey's mobile phone began vibrating on the table. He glanced at his father, who nodded. He grabbed the phone anxiously.

"Status?" He went silent as he listened to the response. "How long ago? How many were there? Any other details on their identities? OK. Did you connect with the compound? Was anything missing? I need answers by noon eastern, got it?" He hung up.

Jefferey turned to his father as he placed his phone back on the table. "I have good news, and I have bad news. The good news is, LeMaster's Sikorsky was spotted in El Paso the day after the crash. It remained at the airport overnight and left the next day. There are five or six individuals, four of them were men. I should get more on their descriptions later today. Also, we checked the airports closest to

LeMaster's residence and got lucky. Apparently, a day before the attack, a government-owned Lear Jet 75 Liberty landed at Sierra Blanca Regional Airport. It can't be a coincidence. The day following the crash, the jet departed with a flight plan to Andrews Air Force Base."

"And the bad news," inquired Peter Gunderson, tapping his fingers impatiently.

Jefferey cleared his throat. "From what our guy on the ground can tell, there was only one thing missing from the residence and that was a server from inside the saferoom."

"And what was on that server?" pressed his father.

"We don't know yet because he didn't have that kind of access. He's trying to find out for us."

"We need to know that today, Jefferey. The server was in the saferoom because it was sensitive. There could be things on it that lead back to us. We need to know if Typhon has been compromised. Get it done."

"Yes sir," responded the younger man.

"OK. Now, based on what we've learned today, coupled with the fiasco in Chicago and the growing noise at Fort Meade, there is cause to suspect that the NSA is spearheading these activities." Jefferey could see the tension in his father's countenance as he paced back and forth.

His father stopped suddenly. "Bring me up to speed on your Washington trip. I need to understand the bigger picture."

Jefferey told him of his meetings with George Brewer and Senator William Billings, and about the commitments and timelines he'd levied.

His father was shaking his head now. "We need to move the timelines up. We need to contact Krishinko and Von Stemp and let them know that they might be compromised. They both need to go dark. Krishinko needs to get back here immediately. We need him close. He'll have to be very careful about how he travels."

"Understood," Jefferey replied. "You should know that I spoke with Krishinko yesterday on my way back from D.C. He called me to report on his meetings with Jasmine Snow in London and Von Stemp in Paris. He was concerned about activities in Europe that could be perceived as a highjacking of our strategy, an attempt to morph it into something else. Perhaps an effort to reverse it, even. And there have been complications in dealing with individual EU countries. He decided to curtail his trip to Tehran and Hong Kong and return early to meet with us to determine how best to deal with these issues. So, he is already on his way. He's going to meet with Abdul and Chenzi via secure VTC from the jet. We'll have his report when he gets here."

"OK. Send a car to meet him at the jet. There can be no situation where someone suspects he's traveled to the U.S."

After Jefferey left to follow up with Brewer, Billings and the missing server, Peter left the kitchen for his wood paneled study. He sat in a plush leather office chair and pressed a smooth panel on the wall to his right. A large flat panel display and keyboard rose out of the floor in front of him.

Gunderson placed his right index finger on the keyboard's biometric scanner, then looked straight into the screen-mounted camera for facial recognition and retinal scan.

"Pull up all records for Nicholi Krishinko," he commanded.

An image of the Russian appeared instantly on his screen with a personal information summary. Several other tabs appeared near the bottom of the screen. He read the summary and clicked through the various folders of information. Most of it he already knew, but recent events mandated he be cognizant of any connections or details that could be used against Typhon due to a potential compromise.

Nicholi Krishinko was born on May 31, 1984, in St. Petersburg, Russia's second largest city. His childhood was normal enough. Both parents were academics and taught at St. Petersburg University, where Krishinko ultimately attended. He was an outstanding athlete in his youth, excelling in gymnastics first and later, wrestling. He studied Cross-Linguistic Communication and Translation, a linguistic curriculum that required fluency in at least two languages. Krishinko did well and mastered proficiency in English, French and Arabic.

Following graduation, he was recruited by the Ministry of Foreign Affairs in Moscow. Krishinko was assigned to work on policy issues with a focus on the EU and the United States. Over time, he became disillusioned with his country's dysfunctional bureaucracy and its decline as a world power. He met Jefferey Gunderson in 2009 at an EU conference in Brussels, Belgium. The two had dinner. Krishinko drank a bit too much that evening, a situation that resulted, however eloquent, in an unbridled soliloquy about his dissatisfaction with the motherland. The next morning, Jefferey tested his interest in making a radical change in his career path. Two months later, Krishinko joined Typhon. He moved up quickly within the organization to his current position. Being Vice President of Typhon Global Operations made him a key member of Core Typhon.

Gunderson checked his watch and pushed back his chair. As he rose to leave, the active display darkened and the system automatically lowered, silently merging into the walnut surface below.

◆

Hours later, Gunderson, Jefferey, and Krishinko were seated at an eighteenth-century card table imported from Brussels. Like many of the antiques throughout the house, this exquisite piece reminded Gunderson of the reasons for Typhon's existence.

"I trust by now you have updated each other," commented Gunderson. "I'm up to speed on Jefferey's findings, at least up until about an hour ago. Nicholi, tell me about your trip."

"Yes sir," Krishinko replied. He gave a synopsis of his meetings in London and Paris before launching into his video calls.

"I connected with Yakim Abdul in Tehran and Suela Chenzi in Hong Kong by VTC on the flight back. Yakim has made a good deal of progress and the situation in Iran is better than I expected. Pressure from the U.S., sanctions and such, are having significant impact on the stability of their government. With the advent of peace agreements between Israel and other Arab nations, they are becoming increasingly isolated. Much of the unrest in Iran has been driven by the younger generations, the Ayatollah and the Imams are increasingly frustrating older segments of the population. So, right in line with Typhon's strategy. Unlike Shariah Muslim movements elsewhere, the people of Iran are moving in a more secular direction. If this continues, Typhon's position will continue to strengthen.

"Hong Kong is another story. They are in a revolutionary state. The Chinese are crushing them, and they have little chance to make any headway. In this case, Typhon has only one play, and that is to play the white knight once Typhon is globally dominant. China will withdraw when faced with overwhelming opposition from the entire international community, and the citizens of Hong Kong will welcome Typhon as a savior. We will use this approach with some of the other weaker nations as well. In summary, the Middle East and Asia are tracking. For the former, we will need some help to mitigate some of the difficulties we are experiencing."

"Good, thanks Nicholi," Gunderson responded flatly. "It is heartening that we have fully half the world progressing according to plan. I would like, however, to table the regional discussion for now. We can pick it back up this afternoon. I believe your recommendations for the UK and the EU are workable. For the EU, it's a matter of mapping the countries' common environments to a series of appropriate responses, then to execute them. With the UK, we should send in a team to take out problematic leadership. That should spin the Brits into an even deeper crisis, which will then open the door to making Typhon's success more assured."

"My immediate concern is right here in the U.S. Jefferey, any more word from your sources on this ground team?"

"Yes, actually. I talked a to our operative in New Mexico. Our guy was able to sneak into LeMaster's underground computer room. It turns out the missing server is the one with all his financial records, contracts and legal documents, business arrangements and equity stakes, and all his media connections and contact information. I've been told no one would ever be able to break into those files because they can only be accessed via LeMaster's bioscan. Fingerprint or whatnot. On top of that, it's all encrypted."

"So they say," responded Gunderson. "Something tells me LeMaster's encryption won't scare the NSA. And his saferoom was also secured via bioscan locks, but they managed to gain entry."

"Point taken," said Jefferey humbly.

"What about the team itself?" Gunderson continued. "Who the hell are they?"

"Some progress, no names yet, but we managed to get several images of them from security cameras at the hotel where they stayed," answered Jefferey. "They were clearly trying to avoid detection, so none of the shots are dead-on, no clear, complete stills but we have software that combines multiple shots. That will hopefully give us some clean images. Once we have those, we can run them through our facial recognition program. We'll be done with that later tonight."

Gunderson nodded and turned to Krishinko. "Tell me about your and Von Stemp's interactions with LeMaster. Do we have anything to worry about?"

"OK. Well, in his original role working both the UK and EU, Von Stemp did a ton of work influencing the media. That was one of the reasons we recruited LeMaster to begin with. He was one of the few people on the planet that could affect media positions worldwide. He interacted with Von Stemp personally on numerous occasions."

"And you?" Gunderson prodded.

"I had limited contact with him, once when I had to authorize a large expenditure, two other times when I needed to intervene for a time-critical requirement."

"Do you know if LeMaster documented any of your or Wart's personal information, or about your meetings with him?"

Krishinko took a moment and then answered reluctantly. "I would have to say that is likely."

Peter Gunderson had anticipated as much and knew what had to be done. "OK then. We need to take out this team before they can do any more damage, and before they have time to ID any more of us. For now, we must assume they will soon know about you and Von Stemp. Identifying either of you could lead them to me, and Typhon won't survive that. Jefferey, get whatever intel you can get from your D.C. sources. Find out who they are, find out where they are right now, and find out what they are planning. We need to know if they've cracked LeMaster's encryption, and if so, what they have learned. We'll meet back here tomorrow at 10:00 am to complete our planning. Then I want you and Nicholi on the jet by 2:00 pm."

They both nodded.

"Good. I'll provide whatever resources you need, just let me know. We've been down this path before. It's not your first rodeo, so get to it and get it done."

CHAPTER EIGHTEEN

CROSSING PATHS

Just one hundred twenty miles on interstate 95 separated Typhon's hit team in Philadelphia and Team Apogee in Washington. Less than a dozen individuals who could change the fate of billions, one way or the other. To the rest of the world, it was a day like any other.

As Mac and Franklin were completing their briefing with Admiral Clausen, Peter Gunderson was reviewing the latest intel from Washington. Brewer had reported in earlier that morning. He'd managed to confirm the existence of a specific federal initiative connected with the NSC. He'd also determined that there was a ground operations team working directly for the NSA Director's office and led by a field operative and ex-Navy Seal named Mac Sisco.

After meeting with Jefferey, Billings assigned two of his aids to conduct a search for off-record NSA projects. They were able to find recent, classified NSC communications and meeting agendas referencing a project launched months earlier codenamed *Apogee*. He also discovered that within the last two weeks, Apogee had been expanded to include most of the NSC Principals Committee members. But there was no change in their activity or schedules that would implicate their involvement. Just hours earlier, a Treasury Department informant told him of a series of impromptu audits on Wall Street that were disconnected from any routine plans of record. The Senator could hardly contain his excitement. Then he hit pay dirt—a texted image of a Top-Secret document listing six names, all part of the 'Apogee Set Team.' Jefferey had been right. The NSA had launched an illicit operation. And it appeared the operation was specifically being shielded from the President.

◆

The NSA Lear 75 was spinning up its engines for its flight to the Caribbean with a quick stop in the Big Apple as Mac and Joe met one final time with Admiral Clausen before their departure later that afternoon.

The Admiral greeted them warmly as they entered the Director's conference room.

"My executive assistant will give today's ops briefing, since he has been working closely with our Agency folks downstairs. Go ahead, Martin," Clausen motioned.

"Thank you, Admiral. Gentlemen, you have already been made aware of two individuals identified in James LeMaster's secure files as Nicholi Krishinko and Wart Von Stemp. We've concluded there is an unnamed parent organization with which they appear to be affiliated. Our analysts have been scouring our databases, the dark web, and the internet non-stop since yesterday to gain details about who they are, how they are involved in LeMaster's illicit activities, and what they are currently up to." Stabler went on to describe the backgrounds and profiles of the two. "While the details around their current activities are sketchy at best," Stabler continued, "one thing about these men has become apparent; they are both elite fighters who should be considered armed and extremely dangerous. In your packet you will find their contact information and all the details I've just briefed to you. Their last known whereabouts is Paris, France.

"One final and very important development before I conclude," Stabler went on. "Yesterday evening, we identified another individual by decrypting their name from a recent text message from LeMaster to Von Stemp. Here is the text." Stabler clicked to the next slide.

Will update you on UK media after NK/JS mtg in L, after my mtg with NK, 23 Hôtel PM at 1700, WVS

"After consultation with Five Eyes, we believe Krishinko recently met with an MI-6 agent named Jasmine Snow in London before traveling to Paris to meet with Von Stemp at the Hôtel Particulier Montmartre. This is a wrinkle…MI-6 may have a mole. Our query was generic enough not to tip off our ally. We won't take even the smallest risk that might jeopardize your operation. Take this into consideration as you move forward, and don't assume U.S. agencies are immune to the same."

As Stabler was wrapping up, Clausen intervened. "Team, nothing from this briefing changes the timeline of our mission. We can't afford to slow down, and we need all activities to continue in parallel. What it does do, as Martin emphasized, is add a wrinkle to our execution. We are in the process of gathering what we can on Jasmine Snow. If this thing—and for lack of a better term we will call them Typhon for now—has infiltrated allied intelligence agencies, we need to trace that and see where and how high it goes. If they have access to NATCOG files and intelligence, it means we are at a serious disadvantage."

"Understood," responded Mac, frowning.

"So," the Admiral continued, "we proceed as planned, except you will fly to London first. Once you are there, I want you to locate and collect what you can on Snow. Your directive and the details are in your packet. Joe, you will leave Mac there and head to Paris and find Von Stemp and Krishinko. Get what you can from them, try to turn them. If that doesn't work, neutralize them. Remember, this is war. We don't have an option to extradite, or the resources to rendition them by force. If things get too dicey, wait for Mac to join you. Any questions?"

Both men shook their heads.

"OK. If you have some time later, you can get in touch with me directly. And I want to emphasize—you two might be able to break this whole thing wide open if you can turn one or both of them or get them back here for interrogation. Stay connected to the rest of the team, and with me. There are a lot of moving parts. When your mission is complete, reconnoiter with the rest of team Apogee. Good luck, and Godspeed."

CHAPTER NINETEEN

ENTANGLEMENT

How far out are we?" Mac asked groggily, squinting as he awoke.

"About two hours now." Joe answered without looking up, busily poring over his FACET Briefing book.

"I guess I needed that," yawned Mac.

"I just can't sleep on planes," commented the big Seal. "It must be something to do with my anxiety about blasting through the air at 30,000 feet and 600 miles per hour, in a heavy metal tube that shouldn't even be able to get off the ground."

Mac laughed, "Yeah, I guess that's a lot worse than working months at a time in a heavy steel tube hundreds of feet underwater."

"Touché," laughed his friend.

"So, what do you think about this whole thing Mac?" asked Franklin.

"I think we're going to have to be very, very careful on this op. I spent some quality time looking at our target's profiles. These guys are nasty. We can't underestimate them."

"Agreed. Von Stemp is a brute, and Nicholi is no slouch."

"Surprise is our friend on all three of these targets," Mac responded.

"That and a nine mil," quipped Joe.

"Let's review the plan one last time before we land," said Mac. "Once we land in London, I will deplane and head into the city to locate Snow. You leave within the hour for Paris, rent a car and check out the hotel where Krishinko and Von Stemp met. Then you will recon Von Stemp's residence, get inside and wait for him to return. Same plan for Krishinko. I will follow Snow from MI-6 headquarters. When the time and place is right, I'll introduce myself and we'll have a chat. Hopefully, we'll both be finished in three to four days. Your assignment has more variables though, Krishinko could be anywhere."

"Copy all," Joe answered.

Mac continued. "If either of us run into trouble, let the other know immediately."

"Five by five," said Joe as they descended.

It was 10:00 am as he pulled his Mini Cooper rental into the lot down the street from the SIS Building at Eighty-Five Albert Embankment in Vauxhall. The Agency had kept a tight bead on Snow's whereabouts since discovering her potential entanglement with Typhon. NSA Intel indicated that she was not currently on an assignment and should be working at the headquarters building. She was described in her profile as a creature of habit. Weather permitting, she routinely took a stroll along the Vauxhall Bridge, eating her lunch on the go. The weather today was pleasant, with a slightly overcast sky and a relatively warm breeze coming off the water of the River Thames. Mac took up a casual position on the riverbank opposite the headquarters building and waited. Just an hour later, he noticed a slim figure break away from a group exiting the main entrance. She clutched a brown paper bag in her left hand and walked briskly towards the bridge. Several pedestrians were on the bridge taking in the picturesque view, some leaning on the rustic reddish railings, others strolling along its wide walkways. As she continued across, he was able to make a positive ID.

Snow welcomed the warm breeze from across the river. Her thick black hair was swept backward as the wind ruffled her light tan jacket. As she approached the far end of the bridge, she noticed a tall, attractive man leaning casually against the railing. Snow spent years profiling people, and she didn't miss much. It was a critical skill in her line of work, one that had saved her life on more than one occasion. It had become an automatic practice to notice when something, or someone, was off.

She scanned the man from the corner of her eye. He had an interesting look. Ray Ban Aviator sunglasses, brown leather bomber coat, slim fitting blue jeans and full quill, peanut butter colored cowboy boots. Short auburn hair hanging loosely over his forehead, and a strong, angular jawline that reminded her of so many male models. His upper body was broad and powerful. As she reached the end of the bridge, he pushed off the railing and began walking towards her. A mild dose of adrenalin hit her veins, but no alarm bells went off. She couldn't see his eyes, but his demeanor was relaxed. His gait was normal. As their paths converged, he smiled and spoke to her.

"Excuse me Ma'am for interrupting you, but I couldn't help notice that you just left that big building across the bridge."

Then the alarm bells went off. "I'm sorry? How can I help you?"

"Well," he continued, "I know this sounds crazy, but I have always been a big fan of Ian Fleming and his James Bond novels, and I understand that building is the headquarters of MI-6, the one in all the Bond books."

This was not a new conversation for Snow. When friends got to know her, they eventually found out where she worked. She too was a Fleming fan, and as young girl had often romanticized about working in intelligence. Then she smiled to herself. *I did not come in with yesterday's rain.*

It was cute. "Yes sir, you are correct, but you need to work on your pickup lines."

The man laughed nervously. "Yeah, I guess you're right. But I really am a huge fan of James Bond." With that, he grinned broadly. "I do apologize for being so forward. But I just can't help myself. Mind if I walk with you a bit?"

She found herself taken, both by his audacity and his charm. "Well alright, so let's walk and talk. My name is Jasmine."

Mac and Snow strolled along the river, chit-chatting and amicably sharing their favorite 007 scenes.

After a while, Snow told him she had to get back to work, adding, "What is your name?"

"Bond, James Bond," he replied in a deep voice. They both laughed. "Sorry I couldn't resist. My name is Mac Sisco. I'm from Austin, Texas."

"Of course you are," she grinned. "I'm Jasmine Snow, and I'm from right here in London." The two laughed again.

Mac touched her arm as she turned to head back to work. "I'd like to take you to dinner, Jasmine. Tonight?"

Normally, she would reject such an offer out of hand. But there was something about this Mac Sisco from Austin that intrigued her. And it had been a while since she'd had any time for romantic interplay. She could use something to take her mind off things.

"That sounds nice."

They agreed to meet, and Mac turned to walked to his car. He was pleased with how it went. She bought his lines and didn't appear worried about his intentions. Quite the opposite, in fact. That said, he knew from her profile that she was an experienced operator with robust counterintelligence training. She could be difficult to read. There were no tells that anything was amiss. And it was a bonus that she was drop dead gorgeous. What a shame that she was on the wrong side. Well tonight would tell. Tempus Fugit. During a good meal and perhaps dessert, he would feel her out and determine his best course of action.

◆

Joe Franklin was accustomed to solo ops. He preferred it, actually, because that way he didn't have to save anyone, just his own ass. But that didn't apply to Mac. While he'd been Franklin's student in another life, nowadays Mac was the only operative Franklin could always rely on, 100 percent of the time. Mac had bailed Franklin out of tight spots more than once. They were truly brothers in arms. For that reason, he didn't like being separated on this mission. Even so, as Franklin arrived at Von Stemp's address, he was confident and focused on the operation.

The Typhon agent kept a two-bedroom corner apartment on the Left Bank of the Seine, almost directly across from the Louvre. Franklin drove slowly by, made a U-turn and parked a block down with a good view of the front door. Then he settled in. After three hours with no indication Von Stemp was home, he decided to take a closer look. He got out of the car and walked down a cross street, then turned left down a lane that ran behind the building. Each apartment on the first level had a small patch of yard behind it surrounded by wrought iron and brick. He continued to the end of the lane, arriving at the opposite cross street with the back entrance to Von Stemp's apartment and immediately to his left.

His little backyard patch was different than the rest, with an eight-foot granite wall and a stone arch entrance with a heavy wood door. He noticed no one in the vicinity, so he approached the door and pulled on the handle. Locked. Then he stepped back and pulled out his phone, pretending to check his bearings. He looked around casually again. Then he moved backwards, took two broad steps and jumped upwards, his right foot on the door handle. From there he launched himself straight up, grasped the top of the granite precipice and dropped quietly down into shadow on the other side. He crept along the wall to the corner of the apartment, where he stopped to listen.

The back entrance to the apartment led out onto a slate patio with cushioned outdoor furniture neatly arrayed around a stone fire pit.

Classic German fastidiousness, thought Franklin, everything neat as a pin. Before moving closer, he examined every part of the perimeter, looking for alarm sensors, trip wires, or motion detectors. There were several cameras strategically placed high along the outside of the house, so he made sure to shield his face and might have to deal with that later.

Franklin took his lock kit from his backpack, which included a series of stainless-steel pics for manual entry and a slim pen-like device with thin steel rods protruding from the end. The automated lock pick was an NSA invention for use with electronic locks that stymied the average agent. Franklin tossed it back in the kit, grabbed his trusty manual tools and went to work. Thirty seconds later, he heard the satisfying click of the lock disengaging and quietly pushed the door inward.

He found himself in a tiny mudroom where he once again stopped to listen. Again, he heard nothing. The hallway led to a traditional French kitchen. It was immaculately clean and finished with modern white cabinets along most of the wall space. A square butcher-block table with a tall wicker chair on each side graced the center of the room. Two rooms opened off the kitchen, one a domed-ceiling dining room with a view of the back yard. The other was a living room furnished with two contemporary black leather couches and a lounge chair.

The rooms were all painted bone white and sported modern impressionist artwork. *Nice digs*, Franklin thought. Then he turned toward a set of stairs and ascended to the second floor. The upstairs hallway ran the length of the apartment, with two doors on each side and one at the end. All closed.

He put his ear to the first door and heard nothing. As he turned the brass knob carefully, he muttered "screw it" under his breath, threw open the door and scanned the room. Nothing but a neatly made contemporary king-sized bed and a matching chest of drawers with a flat screen TV perched on top and an open door to the bathroom. He moved rapidly to the next room, and the next. The last two were a guest bedroom and laundry room. But no sign of Von Stemp.

Franklin was the kind of man who preferred direct confrontation. Stealth was just a necessary step to that end. However, he also liked to optimize the odds of a positive outcome. He wanted Von Stemp to be as surprised as possible. And his SPECOPS experience had given him a lot of insight into these kinds of engagements.

Seals are often faced with missions that require sneaking into well-guarded areas and subduing guards and enemies along the way. They often complete their mission in near silence; women and non-combatants often sleep through the entire thing only to awake the next day to an unsettling scene.

After some thought, he decided his best play was to stake out his quarry from the second floor. He guessed that when Von Stemp returned home he would go to his bedroom to change, and that is when Franklin planned to introduce himself.

CHAPTER TWENTY

SECOND CHANCES

Snow was mildly excited as she entered her apartment at 6:00 pm that evening. This was rare for her because it was a different kind of excitement. She felt almost flushed as she hung up her jacket with the sun's dying rays casting long shadows through the French doors and across the foyer. She smiled as she entered her bedroom, imagining the possibility of an evening devoid of stress, perhaps even a thoroughly enjoyable one.

The muted buzz of her cell phone brought her back to reality. She laid her purse on the bureau, took her phone from her purse, and saw she had a text from work. She scanned it quickly. Her brow furrowed as she read the text a second time.

T may have been compromised by U.S. agent Mac Sisco, NSA. Keep up guard. Crit- KIT, WVS

Suddenly, what she'd hoped would be a casual adventure turned into a crisis. If U.S. intelligence had somehow discovered her, they could try to use or turn her, she could go to prison. Her life would be over. Even though they were strong allies, this sort of thing still happened from time to time. Her head was swimming as she considered her options. She glanced again at her watch. She was supposed to meet with him in a little less than an hour and a half. That didn't give her much time to come up with a plan. Her heart was racing as she willed herself to calm down and do what she did best, think this problem through and find a solution.

At first glance, her options appeared limited. She could disappear immediately and be on the run for the rest of her life. Or admit guilt and take the hit. Imprisonment or worse. Or…eliminate the immediate risk by taking out the threat. None of these options were appealing, and she really didn't know what the Americans had on her, if anything. She needed to know more and that meant playing along for now. Once she had a better understanding of her predicament, she could decide on her next steps. That said, she needed to know how Typhon wanted her to proceed before she met Sisco for dinner.

She keyed a text to Von Stemp.

If U.S. intel ground team contact occurs, what is engagement protocol?

She hit send. Fifteen minutes later as she toweled off after a quick shower, her mobile buzzed again. She left the bathroom and moved to her bedroom nightstand to read the text. Von Stemp replied to her promptly, but her relief was short-lived as she read the response.

Interrogate, terminate & report back

Snow was stunned. Terminate. This directive would make her a murderer. Even if she did what Von Stemp told her to do, she was now a liability to Typhon. There was a high probability they would send a hit team soon after to eliminate her. Unconscionably, prison might be the preferable choice...

Even as she fought off her anger, she began to see a lifeline that Typhon's radical directive had inadvertently provided, a silver lining of sorts. Typhon had seemed the perfect salve for the wound to her country perpetrated by her government's corruption. Typhon represented itself as the savior for the UK's horrid immigration issues and subordination to incompetent EU bureaucrats. They promised a return to the political gentility and self-governance she remembered from her youth.

The directive was a clear manifestation of her fears. Not only was it readily apparent that she was expendable, but the leadership of Typhon must have been both arrogant and naive to believe she wouldn't see the end game. Now, as she formulated her plan, she was left with the painful realization that she had been deceived. The cure was worse than the disease. It had been a big mistake to sign on with Typhon. She had to do what she could to fix it.

Sergio's was among London's finest Italian restaurants. The menu and wine selection were exquisite. It was located on Great Titchfield Street, just five kilometers from Vauxhall Bridge. Mac arrived a few minutes early to ensure their table was as private as possible. Being a weekday, the outdoor seating was not crowded, and he was shown to a semi-secluded table away from the entrance. Mac wore tan slacks, a black turtleneck under a dark brown cashmere sports coat, and his peanut butter boots.

He ordered a glass of pinot noir and waited patiently for Snow to arrive. Although he appeared relaxed as he leaned back in his cushioned wrought iron chair, Mac was on the alert. He casually scanned the diners, looking for incongruities. Things that were off. Nothing caught his eye until Jasmine Snow approached, along the sidewalk and over to his table. Her red silk dress fluttered, cinched at the waste by a black alligator belt. She wore a black shawl with tasseled ends draped over her shoulders. She was beautiful. More like a runway model than an intelligence agent, but he wasn't complaining.

"Good evening, Jasmine, you look ravishing," Mac said as he stood to pull out her chair.

She smiled appreciatively. "You don't look so bad yourself, cowboy."

The waiter approached as she settled in and took her drink order, a glass of Chardonnay.

Once her drink arrived, Mac raised his glass. "Here's to second chances."

She regarded him quizzically. "*Second* chances?"

He winked at her. "I had a date recently that didn't go well."

"So, this is a date then?" Snow said coyly.

"That was my intention…let's roll with it for now."

They both ordered the linguini and cream sauce with mussels, scallops, and shrimp. Tiramisu with vanilla gelato for dessert. Knowing Mac's true identity and intentions gave Snow an edge, as he did not know that she knew. But it resulted in conversation that was kept light and guarded.

"I have to say, Jasmine, Sergio's is a keeper. I can't remember a better Italian dining experience," Mac said sincerely.

"Well Mac, on that we certainly agree. It's my favorite spot in London."

"If you don't mind my asking, is the real thing anything like the Bond books?"

Snow was almost frustrated at this point. She'd already resigned herself to letting Mac break the ice—to drop the hammer on her and her association with Typhon. But it appeared as if he was enjoying this. Was he getting what he could from her, before he takes everything? She continued playing his game.

"Now Mac, you know if I answer that I would have to kill you," she shot back with a wink. "But I will tell you this, it's certainly not as glamorous."

"Really…how so?"

"It's mostly paperwork and research. Surely, you should know that…"

The end of her reply made him pause. "Yes, I guess that's true of a lot of businesses these days." What a strange thing for her to say… But I read that you guys are out in the field all the time. Don't you have to do some of that?"

Here it comes, Snow mused. *He is beginning to dig. But he just gave me the perfect segue.* "Occasionally," Jasmine continued, "but the trickiest assignments are undercover operations, and those come with a lot of research and analysis. If you skimp on the preparation, the operation fails." She continued before he could redirect her. "What really complicates things is, sometimes you must do some of that preliminary work, even field engagement, before telling the organization. You know, to make sure you're not bringing the Agency a false flag. You must validate things first. It's like being a journalist—you have to corroborate the details before saying you have a story."

"Whoa," Mac responded, wondering what she was getting at. "If you operate that way, you wouldn't have any back up, would you? Is that normal operating procedure? Why would you do that?"

"There are several reasons. One, you must protect your CI's." "What's that," he feigned?

She cringed, wishing the game were over. "Confidential Informants. If they are exposed, they could be hurt or even die, depending on the situation."

"Got it," he responded.

"Another, issue, while rare, is when management doesn't want you to pursue an investigation—even though it is real, and urgent, and pursuit of it that leads to a successful conclusion will benefit the country."

She was acting strange. Saying way more than she should. She was up to something. It felt *off*. "Now wait a minute, why wouldn't your superiors want you to pursue a case like that?"

"Mac, there are more reasons than I can tell you and some that I can't even disclose, but suffice to say, it happens. The bottom line is, I have had to stick my neck out a long way sometimes to see a case through."

Mac was at critical decision point. Snow's answers indicated that she might very well be involved in an undercover operation *against* this Typhon organization—and not colluding with them. It was also possible MI-6 was not yet aware of her activities—though that would be an unlikely scenario. If true, Snow might not be guilty of anything other than conducting a rogue undercover op that could end up being crucial to taking these guys down. It also meant that he couldn't expose her to MI-6, which would risk blowing the op and maybe her career. There was also another possibility of course and that was that somehow, she had made him and was laying down a cover story.

Snow interrupted his train of thought as he paid the server. "Hey, I took a cab here. Would you mind giving me a lift home? My flat is only a couple kilometers away."

"I'd love to. I'm parked just down the street. Ready to go?"

She nodded as she pushed her chair. Fifteen minutes later he pulled the Mini Cooper over in front of her apartment. Mac walked around, opened her door, and offered his hand. As she stepped out their physical proximity stirred something in her. It was frustrating that she was attracted to him—she couldn't let her guard down. But maybe she could use it to her advantage? Something told her Mac was a better agent than that, but she would keep it in her hip pocket.

"Well," she said while feigning her best awkward smile, "it's still early, do you fancy a nightcap?"

Mac was wondering if it had ever been this easy. *I guess I still got it.* "I'd love to," he answered.

Snow saved him from going to plan B. If she had not offered, Mac would have asked. But as it turned out, he didn't have to, and it was time to get to the truth.

Moments later, they were sitting across from each other in upholstered wingback chairs in front of a red brick fireplace, sipping cognac from crystal tulip glasses. Then Mac began.

"Jasmine," he said, "I'd like clear some things up."

She nodded apprehensively. *Here it comes*, she thought.

He went on. "First, I know I was very vague when you asked me what I did for a living. I'm not in the international oil consulting business. The truth is, I'm a special agent with American Intelligence."

Now Snow's eyebrows furrowed, and her lip curled a bit. Her tone was sharp. "I suspected something was off. You were too smooth. Everything was too perfect. Now tell me, as one intelligence professional to another and without any more bloody BS, why are you trying to play me?"

Mac took it in stride. "We have intel you may be engaged with an international terrorist cabal that is fomenting cultural and societal upheavals on a global scale. I am here to verify that, and to see if we might come to an understanding."

An understanding… "I see," responded Snow, unemotionally. "That's quite an accusation, Mac. I'm going to have to see your credentials."

Mac nodded and held out his badge.

"NSA, hmm…this is not your usual playground."

"You'd be surprised, Jasmine. Now, my question."

Still on edge, she corrected him immediately. "It was a statement, there was no question."

Mac sighed. "Let me rephrase. Are you involved in any way with such an organization?" he asked.

"Yes I am."

Her abrupt acknowledgement surprised him. "Do they have a name, and what is the nature of your involvement with them?"

"They are called Typhon. They sought me out about nine months ago after someone within the organization perceived I had one or more professional difficulties at SIS. They thought these alleged vulnerabilities were effective kompromat and began to recruit me. They promoted themselves as a well-funded and legitimate NGO. The bottom line is, Mac, you are now interfering with an MI-6 undercover operation. The only reason I'm telling you anything is so the NSA doesn't get their wires crossed and screw this up for us."

Mac was taken aback but pressed for more. "OK, let's assume all that is true. Can you tell me how you got involved, and again, can you tell me what your current role is with them?"

"I can give you a little more. I had already completed significant research to try and identify what the international catalysts were for the systemic disruptions we've been experiencing in the UK," she continued. "It was that work that allowed my path to cross with theirs, and they made initial contact. A man named Wart Von Stemp interviewed me. I was able to convince him of my loyalty and commitment to their cause, and they brought me in. Because of my position with MI-6, they made me what they call their 'UK Commissar.' While I have had success penetrating their organization, they are very compartmented, and I have not yet uncovered enough actionable intel to disclose my op to my superiors. Yes, you could say this is a rogue operation if you want but we are not the CIA, or the NSA. We do things differently here."

"Just like James Bond," Mac quipped, unconvinced. He couldn't take the chance she might decide to work as a double agent. The problem was, how to validate her claims? He had to test her somehow, force her to expose the truth in a way that was irrefutable.

He decided to be unapologetically direct. "Jasmine, your story is very interesting, but we still have a problem."

She nodded. "You can't be sure I am telling the truth, so you must treat me as an opponent. That means taking me off the board until you can collect the evidence one way or the other."

"Exactly," he said. "So, help me out, how can you prove to me that what you're saying is true?"

Snow paused before answering. "There really is only one way, Mac. Bring me into your operation. Let me help you work against Typhon, to shut them down and bring them in. This will help me as well—I can then bring what I know back to MI-6. This could even become a joint operation."

"I am not sure my colleagues would agree with that plan," Mac answered.

"Why not? The risk is low. You control the op, the resources, the assignments, and the intel. You can leverage my career if you like. I would have no choice but to deliver."

"Jasmine, you may be a good intelligence officer, but no one in their right mind—only someone already in deep water would recommend what you just did. It's clear to me you are in trouble, and this is your only way out."

She tilted her head to one side sullenly. "I…got in deeper than I wanted to. I should have reported what I knew earlier. If I take what I know about Typhon to headquarters now, I'll be booted from MI6. At best. I don't know how to fix this. Maybe there's still some way for me to make it out of this mess unscathed."

Mac took a sip of cognac and felt it's warmth course down his throat. His plan had been to learn as much as possible about Typhon from Snow. She would either provide the information willingly, or he would subdue her and take her into custody for interrogation. He was also authorized to eliminate her if she presented an immediate threat. It would seem she was opting for the former.

"OK Jasmine. Let's feel this out. Tell me how you think this might go down. If you can convince me that you have something of value to bring to the table, then I will see what I can do for you."

"Fair enough." She exhaled nervously. "I'm comfortably certain I have far more intel about Typhon than the NSA, as it pertains to the UK. I have direct access to some of their operators. I can create a convergence."

"Convergence? You mean entrapment?"

"Yes," she said. "After a period of time collecting, I can set it up, a meeting or whatever, maybe with Von Stemp and others. You can roll in and collect them, rendition them back to the U.S.

Mac didn't trust her. Everything she was saying screamed that she was simply trying to keep from getting caught. From going to jail, or worse. "That would be a beneficial outcome. For the U.S., and for the U.K. I like where you're going with this but let's be clear, if we did this you would operate strictly according to our protocols. You would wear a wire at all times. No deviations from our direction. Would you agree to that?"

She nodded. "I'm Ok with all that, but I do have one request."

"You're not in a position to be making requests, don't you think? What is it?"

"If your instructions violate my organization's policies or my personal ethics, I have the right to refuse," she answered.

Mac thought on it before responding. "I would agree to the former, but not the latter. Personal ethics have no real place in tradecraft," he said flatly. "They vary from person to person and tend to get in the way of the mission."

Snow regarded him silently, then relented. The tension evaporated as they both realized that, at least for now, they were on the same team. Snow stood up and grabbed the cognac bottle.

"Shall we drink to our new partnership?"

Mac grinned. "Why not."

Snow poured two fingers in each glass. Mac stood with her, and they raised their glasses together.

"To second chances," she offered, and touched his glass. She gazed into his eyes and asked softly, "OK cowboy, where do we go from here?"

Her eyes were almost pleading. He could smell her perfume. This had all been too easy. A hundred warning bells went off in his head as he touched her free hand with his. She didn't flinch or withdraw, but gently took his hand as if to say, *it's ok, we both want this*. Guiding him into her bedroom, she dimmed the light and he lowered her onto the quilt-covered king-sized bed. Mac kissed her cheek gently and whispered in her ear, *"I think this is going to work out just fine..."*

CHAPTER TWENTY-ONE

TAKE NO PRISONERS

Von Stemp was leaving his office when he received and responded to Snow's text. Her question concerned him greatly, and he was still trying to decide what he might do. It could take months to replace her, and this was no time for rearranging the hierarchy. He had to wait until she submitted her report. However, this sort of predicament was the part of his job that he thirsted for. He'd always been an adrenaline junky. Things like this just didn't happen enough.

The thrill of the hunt, the danger. The risk and the realization that so much was at stake were what made his various termination assignments so gratifying. Von Stemp knew as sure as the sun would rise tomorrow that at some point, they were going to come for *him*. They could already be on their way. They probably already knew where he lived, what restaurants frequented, the pubs he favored. He was a pro; he knew what to expect. *Let the games begin…*

As he exited the EU's Paris Field underground parking garage, he began his surveillance. He would return home to retrieve his gear and set up his defenses. There was one, maybe two agents coming for him. That was manageable. He held the edge because he knew they were coming. As he pulled out, he scanned the area. Nothing out of the ordinary caught his eye. But that didn't mean they weren't there. He turned right, heading away from his home. At a specific intersection he entered one of his six evasion routes, one that added an extra thirty minutes. Time enough to either ID or evade a tail.

Forty-five minutes later, Von Stemp rolled slowly to a stop just up the street from his apartment. He hadn't noticed anyone following him. From the glove compartment he pulled out his Sig Sauer P938. With a round in the chamber, he slipped off the safety and tucked the gun in his pants at the small of his back. Then he got out, pressed the door closed and started down the sidewalk, making a left down the side street and approaching from the back of the complex. He stopped fifty meters out to scan the windows, then moved quickly up to the large wooden door protecting the rear entrance.

As Von Stemp inserted the key into the door, he noticed something he hadn't noticed before. The handle was ever so slightly askew. He turned the key. The key turned, but with more friction than normal.

There was little question in Von Stemp's mind that the handle had been tampered with. Someone may have broken into or could be in his apartment right now. If someone was inside waiting for him, they could have already gone through his things. Found the best place inside to ambush him. He would prefer to draw them out, but he couldn't risk a shootout that everyone in the neighborhood could hear and see.

Joe Franklin was beginning to wonder if he had called it wrong. Maybe Von Stemp wasn't coming home tonight. Maybe he was already on the run and thousands of miles away. Maybe Franklin should have staked out the EU HQ building, waited for Von Stemp to leave, and then followed him. Maybe Von Stemp was on to him and had a plan to turn the tables. Had *he* been followed? No, he was sure of that. Had Von Stemp planted someone near the apartment who had observed him enter, and contacted the Typhon agent? That was possible, but he didn't think so. Either way, he couldn't stop the gnawing feeling that something wasn't right.

With his Sig in his right hand, Von Stemp gently unlocked and opened the back door with his left. Before he entered the kitchen, he removed his leather loafers and put on his running shoes, keeping an eye on the hallway. After lacing them tightly, he silently crossed the kitchen and peered around the doorframe. All clear. He moved rapidly now to the living room TV grabbing his home automation remote. He checked the bathroom and hallway closet, then moved to the stairs.

At the second-floor landing, he saw an empty corridor with all doors closed. Just as he had left them. He opened his bedroom door with a thrust, sweeping the Sig right to left. Nothing amiss, no one hiding in the closet. He went back to the hallway and moved to the bathroom. Also empty. Von Stemp then went back to his bedroom, positioning himself just inside the door. He took the remote from his jacket pocket and pressed a button. Seconds later, the sound of voices wafted up from the first floor as the TV came to life. Von Stemp put his ear to the door and listened.

Von Stemp waited. After fifteen minutes, nothing. Either no one was here, or if anyone had come at all they came and left before he arrived. He went to the corridor and checked the other rooms—empty—then went to the closet door at the end of the hall. After unlocking it he opened the large gun safe within and grabbed extra ammo, an AR-15, a nine-inch military assault knife, and a suppressor for his Sig Sauer. He screwed the silencer to the end of the Sig and put the rest into a backpack. He snatched two round bundles of U.S. bills and a stack of passports off the top shelf and tossed them in the bag. He closed the vault door, spun the wheel, and returned to his bedroom to pack some clothes and a few other necessities. He wouldn't be able to return for some time; perhaps never. Finished packing, he went downstairs, turned off the TV and back upstairs.

◆

Forty-five minutes earlier, Joe Franklin was beginning to think his plan would backfire. Von Stemp might know they were on to him. He may never come back, or if he did, he would be extremely cautious. Trying to surprise him in his own home under such circumstances could backfire. He left the apartment as he'd found it, went outside, and took up a position behind a few bushes, diagonally across from the back side of Von Stemp's building. There, he waited patiently in the growing shadows where he had retreated minutes before Von Stemp had arrived. When he saw Von Stemp enter carefully though the back, he realized his suspicions were warranted.

This was his chance to catch Von Stemp unaware. Let him search the place, find nothing amiss, and let his guard down… He waited twenty minutes, then quickly moved to the gate door, eyes on the windows for any movement. Von Stemp had left it unlocked, along with the back door. Probably so he could make a quick exit if necessary. He pulled out his P30 and entered, walking silently to the bottom of the stairs. He could hear tap water running. He crept up silently. At the top, he could see the bedroom door was ajar. He moved to the entrance and looked carefully inside. On the bed he saw a handgun a small stack of clothes, and a backpack. *Planning a little trip, eh?* Von Stemp was in the bathroom, his bare back framed in the doorway. Franklin stepped purposefully into the bedroom, the 9 mm aimed directly between Von Stemp's muscled shoulders.

Sensing movement, Von Stemp raised his head and stared open eyed in the mirror at Joe Franklin and his outstretched semi-automatic.

"Don't move," Franklin cautioned forcefully. "Put your hands on your head. Interlock your fingers. Then turn around slowly and get on your knees."

Without saying a word, Von Stemp seemed to comply. As he began to kneel, however, and without warning, he exploded forward into the air, both arms outstretched.

Franklin realized he'd made a grave error. He was too close, and Von Stemp's trajectory was low. He was not reaching up to disarm him. Instead, he accelerated forward into Franklin's legs before he could lower his aim and fire. Over 200 pounds of muscle and bone crashed brutally into the big Seal's legs, launching him backward to the hardwood floor. The inertia of his attack carried him past Franklin and within arm's reach of the bed and his Sig Sauer.

Von Stemp was on his feet in an instant and lunged for the weapon just as Franklin rolled over and up to his feet. Incredibly, he still held his own weapon, but Von Stemp was already raising his for the kill shot. Franklin dove into the bathroom and scrambled into the tile shower as the first *psst* of a suppressed round flew by inches from his head. Franklin silently cursed himself for his miscalculation. He had completely outmaneuvered the German and yet here he was, stuck in a shower and now Von Stemp had him trapped, just feet away.

"It would seem the tables have turned," Von Stemp stated loudly.

"Mr. Von Stemp," Franklin responded, "I am an agent with Interpol, you are to be detained for questioning. Lay down your weapon and surrender."

"Pathetic," Von Stemp shot back. "Interpol doesn't break and enter private residences. In fact, I think I'll call them right now. Something tells me they won't know who you are."

Shit. Franklin only had one play. He had to charge this guy and somehow avoid getting shot in the process. Or he could continue to stall, keep him talking. He could make a mistake…

At that point, he decided Von Stemp was bluffing. Von Stemp was fleeing, and time was running out. "Mr. Von Stemp, please do call for my reinforcements, as the situation stands, I could use some backup." As he talked, Franklin pushed the bathroom door almost closed, blocking Von Stemp's view. Then he moved from the shower to the Jacuzzi by the window.

Von Stemp wasn't alarmed. This guy had nowhere to go. With one eye on the door, he began jamming his gear and clothes into the backpack. In ten seconds, he was done and ready to make a run for it. Should he risk killing the intruder? Authorities would eventually find a dead man in his bathroom. He didn't have time to try to dispose of a body properly—not in Paris anyway.

Franklin stayed low initially. The steel and ceramic walls of the Jacuzzi would protect him. Then he heard Von Stemp shuffling around in the next room. This might be his only chance. He reached up carefully and unlatched the lock on the sliding window above the tub. Once open, he raised his head enough to get a look through the gap in the bathroom door. He could see the bedroom doorway to the hall and part of the bed, but nothing else.

Franklin went back to the window and pulled himself up and straddled the frame. The sun had set, and it was overcast—very little ambient light. The bedroom balcony was six feet away. *Ok,* thought Franklin, *parkour.* There wasn't anything to hold on to, but he was able to wedge his foot against the window sash while he gripped the inside of the upper frame. He leaned his body clear of the window out into the air and swung both his left leg and arm backward. He pushed off hard with his right foot while swinging towards the railing. As his lower body slammed into the side of the concrete balcony, he was able to reach the railing with both hands and he pulled himself over.

It wasn't graceful and it wasn't silent. He was ready as a round burst through the wall to his left. The curtains were drawn; Von Stemp couldn't see him. *Two can play this game,* he thought. He was probably crouching behind the bed. Franklin crawled on the deck to the sliding glass door, aimed upward for a shot that would hit a target at three feet, and fired off two suppressed rounds through the glass, shattering into a thousand pieces. He immediately scrambled back behind the wall as another hole burst through, dangerously close to his head.

Von Stemp did not want a firefight. His neighbors were going to hear the commotion. This guy was a pro, and his odds were fifty-fifty at best, he figured. He was running out of time. His best bet was to lay down some hard fire and make a break for it.

Live to fight another day was not a Seal motto, but it was advice that made sense in certain situations. Years of counterterrorist engagements had taught Franklin that sound risk management almost always was a winning strategy. To burst blindly into the room hoping to get a lucky shot off before Von Stemp got him was not a sound strategy. So, he waited.

Von Stemp secured his backpack, slung the AR over his shoulder and reloaded his Sig. Then he aimed the Sig at the balcony curtains and pulled off four shots in quick succession. Almost before he got the fourth shot off, he burst towards the open bedroom door and skidded around the corner into the corridor.

After the barrage, Franklin sensed something was off and jumped to the gap in the curtains in time to see Von Stemp race through the door. He raised his gun and fired five shots, each one three feet ahead of the other along the adjoining wall. The rounds exploded through the drywall on the hallway side, sending dust and pieces of gypsum into the air. The fourth round found its mark, hitting Von Stemp in the shoulder. The bullet shattered his scapula and deflected upward into the ceiling.

Von Stemp staggered, almost falling down the stairs as he reached the landing. The pain was excruciating. He grabbed the rail and struggled down to the back door. He'd been shot three times during his escapades with Typhon and knew he'd need professional medical attention. The bleeding was moderate, which meant no serious arterial damage. He had to get to his car, make his escape and attend to the wound. Then he could call for extraction.

Franklin stepped through the shattered glass and pushed aside the curtains. He made his way to the hallway and continued to the stairway. As he started down, he saw droplets of blood on the hardwood. He followed the blood trail to the rear of the apartment. Approaching sirens became audible as he stepped into the backyard. Von Stemp had left the back yard door open. He jogged to his car and drove out of the neighborhood just as three police cars screamed by him, lights flashing.

Von Stemp was gasping for breath as he reached his car. He could hear the distant sirens and wanted to get out of there before they got too close. He felt lightheaded as he started the engine. Flashing lights in the rear-view mirror gunned his adrenaline, and the lightheadedness passed. The police cruiser turned behind him on to his apartment's street, its spotlight serpentining through the neighborhood.

His heart thumped loudly in his chest as he drove away. Exhaling painfully, he held the steering wheel with his injured arm and retrieved his mobile phone from the backpack with his other. He tapped the calculator app, then typed $26.2 + 1 =$. A text screen appeared. He tapped the transcribe icon and spoke his message:

Engagement with U.S. actor at residence, wounded, need medical and extraction stat, will go to SH F1.

He hit send, then tapped another button and a map appeared with numerous green pins positioned throughout France. Each pin was identified with "F" and a number and its address. Von Stemp pressed F1 and started his car. The address popped up on his Nav screen and he slowly pulled out onto the dark street.

CHAPTER TWENTY-TWO

THE HUNT

They were up before the sun. Mac was wondering if he'd made a mistake, or if he'd made a *bad* mistake. *It certainly complicates things,* he thought. He wondered what Clausen would say. He could always tell him what he'd told him before, that it was part of the plan. That he had to 'take one for the team'…

Snow shouted from the shower. "Hey Mac, can you hand me the shampoo? It's on the sink."

Well at least she didn't call him cowboy again. He could rock the look, but he wasn't a cowboy. Far from it, actually. He walked into the bathroom and handed her the bottle around the shower curtain.

"Could you scrub my back for me, cowboy?" She asked playfully.

He rolled his eyes with a smile and joined her.

Later, Mac made eggs, bacon, and English muffins, finishing just as Snow walked in from the bedroom. She was wearing skinny blue jeans, a tight white turtleneck and clunky-looking black leather boots. Her hair was pulled back into a ponytail.

"Wow, thank you, Mac," she exclaimed, seeing his handiwork. "A looker, *and* a cooker."

"Wait 'til you try my French toast. It's to die for. Dig in, we have a lot to do today."

As Snow cleared the table, Mac went to the bedroom to retrieve his cell. "Shit," he whispered as he listened to a voice message from Franklin. He'd put his phone on silent last night and missed three calls from him. He immediately called him back. Franklin picked up after one ring.

"Joe," Mac said, "I just got your voicemail. Are you OK?"

"Five by five," Franklin answered. There was a note of disappointment in his voice. "But things are more complicated now."

"What do you mean? What happened?"

Franklin gave him the blow by blow. "I'm just glad you're OK. For the record, if you were injured and off the board things would be worse. It's not like you were too cautious. That said, Von Stemp is now in the wind. We may have to call off your part of the op, I don't know—we've lost the upper hand. They might send in someone after you. They know what you look like." Mac paused in thought. "You're going to need some help. I'm pretty much done here, and I think I have a plan. I'll bring Snow with me."

"Say what?" replied an astonished Franklin. "You recruited her?"

"In a manner of speaking, yes," answered Mac.

Mac brought him up to speed.

"Mac, it sounds good, but you know we can't trust her, right? She's just trying to save her own ass."

"I think the risk is worth the reward, Joe. But I agree, we need to keep her on a tight leash."

"You profiled her. How are her combat skills?" asked Franklin.

"Dunno, it wasn't in her profile. She must be at least capable, given her job description. I *can* tell you, without a doubt, that she is very fit."

"Mac, you didn't… Did you?"

Mac said nothing, smiling.

"You did, what the fuck were you thinking?"

"Don't worry," Mac said in a hushed tone. "My head is clear. Listen, she's in the next room. We will catch a flight to Paris today and join you by late afternoon. In the meantime, call back to the Agency. They may have some idea about where he might lay low. He was wounded, so he might go to a hospital. Have them check on that. Check on airports in the vicinity—he'd probably be using a private or chartered jet. Use a one-hundred-kilometer radius. I will call Clausen and bring him up to speed. I'll also ask him for some SIGINT resources to help us there. As soon as I have the flight details, I'll give you our ETA."

"Copy that, see you later buddy." Franklin hung up.

◆

Peter Gunderson read Von Stemp's text and turned to his son. "Things are getting out of hand. Wart was just ambushed at his home in Paris. He was shot but managed to get away to one of our safehouses." He was red in the face, containing his anger. "We must accelerate our plans. But first, we need to send someone in to eliminate whoever attacked Wart. It may not be a strategic blow, but it will make them more cautious. Slow them down. We can't let them think they are gaining ground on us."

Jefferey nodded. "Nicholi is landing in Paris soon. I'll have him join Wart at the safehouse. I'll fly there as well. We'll handle it."

"Jefferey, I trust that you will. But God forbid, if you fail, I'll be forced to initiate our failsafe protocol—Chaos. Within seventy-two hours, we will begin Typhon's final phase. It would be premature, but not catastrophically so."

After his son left, Gunderson returned to his office and fired up his computer. He queried the system verbally. "Computer, pull up a list of all our operatives worldwide with their locations and operational status."

"Yes, Mr. Gunderson," it replied in a monotone voice.

He leaned back in his chair and rubbed his eyes. The big screen in front of him filled with data. It was organized first by country and then by name. Each well-paid agent had an assigned geographic region and contact information. It represented decades of work. The network was there to help Typhon surgically manipulate its control across the world and as a contingency, if it was discovered and opposed, they were empowered via Chaos to act independently in response to their own circumstances. Bureaucratic and network disengagement enabled immediate action and precision, and as a bonus, created the illusion that they were nothing more than a number of autonomous, unconnected actors. Not part of a larger group. Much like Bin Laden's Al Qa'ida.

Typhon spent billions of dollars over many, many years establishing the network to gain global control, all under the radar. It was designed in a way that ensured control remained invisible. None of the operatives knew each other, none had met or knew the real name of the person they reported to, and none were privy to Typhon's strategic plans. Gunderson had studied mankind's failed efforts at authoritarianism. Rome fell not because they overextended themselves, but because the people with authority were too visible to the masses. Everyone knew who was in charge. Revolutionists, malcontents—they must have a target. Someone to blame, an enemy they could fight.

Typhon was different. To the people, it didn't exist. It operated behind a curtain, like the Wizard of Oz. Gunderson had no interest in being a messiah or recognized as leader of any kind. He was more than content being the world's puppet master, pulling here, nudging there. Until his new world order vision was realized. After that, he could settle back and live more of a normal life, taking action only when needed to keep that order in line.

He began to scroll through the countries and their agents. Australia. Not a critical country in the grand scheme of things. Lots of geography, but isolated and with a small population. On the other hand, they were a Five Eyes member. His top agent there was one of two Deputy Directors-General of the Australian Security Intelligence Organization, Australia's equivalent of the NSA. Upon initiating Operation Chaos, he was instructed to launch a government inquiry into wrongdoings perpetrated by the Prime Minister and his party to destabilize the government. Gunderson's leverage on the Deputy Director was iron clad. Proof of an ongoing relationship with organized crime, and evidence of a money-laundering scheme in a previous banking position.

He moved down the list until he came to Israel. His main agent there was a member of Shin Bet, Israel's internal security organization. His charge was to assassinate the Prime Minister. It would send the country into a panic and allow other Typhon in country assets to gain significant influence.

Then he skipped to the bottom and selected the United States. America had many regions, organized by various criteria. Government, geography, industry, financial, media, influencers, and technology. Government was by far the best infiltrated with agents at local, state, and federal levels. As impressive as Typhon's reach was into the intelligence community, media and technology were also well penetrated. A broad spectrum of influencers was also on board from sports to entertainment, big tech, even gaming.

Right now, however, he was more concerned with the financial category. It was the epicenter of change. Except perhaps for religious fanaticism, money was the most dominant driving force in the direction of history. Gunderson knew well that anything, and anyone could be bought. Money might even be more of a force than religion. The Pope might even sell his soul, for the right price.

CHAPTER TWENTY-THREE

FOLLOW THE MONEY

Pat Curry and Carrie Swan were busy carrying out their charade as Treasury Department auditors on Wall Street. Their cover was irrefutable since the op was being driven by that very agency. But they had to keep up appearances. They could only request access to appropriate files and passwords, or they might blow their cover.

By the end of the first day, they had come up with very little and were running out of ideas. They were working out of a small office with two metal desks now covered with stacks of files and empty Styrofoam coffee cups.

"I'm running out of ideas," said Swan with unusual pessimism.

"Yep, me too," responded Curry. "If we don't find something soon, we may have to walk away with nothing. We're beginning to outstay our welcome."

"I've searched every server, and nothing," responded Swan. "Everyone here is acting too confident. Everything appears copacetic. We should have found something by now."

"Your right," agreed Curry. "Usually, when the Feds come in for an audit, blood pressure goes up. They should look worried. No one is even asking us how it's going."

"Wait a minute, what did you say?" Swan asked, excited.

Curry, rubbed his chin, "I said, usually when the Feds come in for an audit, people's blood pressure goes up."

"I think that's it, Pat."

The big Aussie smiled broadly. "Yep, I do that often. But, how so?"

"Why would everyone be so confident, like they are here, in the middle of a financial audit?" Swan asked.

"Well, if they'd covered their tracks, I guess," he replied. "Hidden all the evidence."

"Right," answered Swan. "And how would you do that?" she continued.

"Move the data to a place no one would look for it."

"Right again," Swan answered.

"But where would that be?" asked Curry.

"You said that their blood pressure would go up, right? What if they hid everything in a place we are not allowed to look, like in highly confidential medical records? HIPPA laws protect that data from anyone not authorized to review the records. That includes financial auditors."

"That's probably a stretch, Carrie. But let's check it out. We've come up with nothing trying to do this the standard way."

Swan made short work hacking the firm's health records. The challenge now was to identify embedded files that concealed the sensitive financial records. She knew the file names would be bogus to camouflage their true content. But they screwed up when they didn't take the ruse far enough. Rather than attempt to find a needle in a haystack, Swan surmised that, in their paranoia, they might use a second layer of protection on the compromising information, so that is what she looked for. A search for files protected by two levels of authentication, strong passwords, and encryption revealed several unique folders.

"Gotcha," she said out loud.

Curry looked up. "Got something?"

"I think I found the safe. Now we have to crack it," she replied. "I'm sending the details to our team now. Hopefully, they can do the work for us remotely. In the meantime, I'm going to see if there's a back door."

Fifteen minutes later, Swan turned to Curry. "I think I can hack in. This is a standard file structure, and the encryption is nothing extraordinary. It may even be better than using the password if the Agency cracks it because there will be no record of the access..."

Swan's phone buzzed. "Speak of the devil," she exclaimed, scanning the text. "The guys came through. But still... I think I should try first."

Curry agreed Swan's hack was a better option. It would leave no tracks. She would have to do it anyway to create her own back door, which she wanted to do to access files remotely later. That way, they could monitor activity and changes. Two hours later the lights began flickering off ten stories below as employees left for the day and they were reviewing the fruits of her labor.

Curry turned to Swan and whispered enthusiastically, "let's call it a night and send our report from the hotel."

She nodded. "I'll send a message to the boss and let him know we're in." Swan texted just two words to Admiral Clausen:

Gold mine.

Back in their hotel they ordered room service, fired up Swan's laptop, and uploaded the files from her flash drive. They would do a deep dive on the data, encrypt the entire cache, and send it back to the Agency for further analysis.

There were twenty-six folders of files. She began with the first one, named HPort-2020. There were seven files. She clicked one labeled hportglob12020.xlsx. The spreadsheet was one she had looked at briefly back at the firm, but now she carefully examined every field. There were over 500 rows and numerous columns of data. The first column header was CNTRY, the next CA, the third CURR BAL, then FCST BAL. The next few columns were labeled INV1, INV2, and INV3, followed by ACT, TGT, SPND and CMNTS.

Curry was the first to comment. "This includes references to activities. It's a mini financial plan. Revenues coming into Typhon from different investors with current balances and forecasted investments. It lists which countries the money is targeted for within different geographies. The last few columns seem to indicate targets and actions."

"I agree," said Swan. "Take a look at some of these entries. For CNTRY *UK,* it says *MP* under TGT and *ASS* under ACT, with a spend of one million. This would be a reach, but it could mean Typhon has a plan to assassinate a Parliamentary Minister in the UK. The dollar amount makes sense. And look here, in the U.S. row, the 'target' is

John Whitaker, our education executive from Chicago! And the 'action' is *Veto School Choice*. Looks like we just validated all the content in this spreadsheet. Boom."

As the two continued to scan the list, their eyes grew wide as the scope of Typhon's plans began to unfold. "We must get this encrypted and over to Clausen immediately," Swan said urgently. "We can review the rest afterwards."

"I agree. You know, there are a lot of gaps in this file," Curry responded. "There are no dates or timelines. In many cases the TGT field is empty."

"It's probably a work in progress, the file was updated recently," said Swan, "but what we do have here will allow us to counter many of their ongoing plans. We could put Typhon on the defensive. Shut them down and begin to roll them up."

"Your right. And they don't know what we know and that is huge," Curry agreed. "We'll be able to anticipate their moves and act against them proactively."

◆

Fifteen hundred miles away, Singe and Warsaw were in the third day of their conference on Grand Cayman Island with mixed results. A cocktail party mixer the first night where they met a few of their target bankers, conversations that enabled them to get their foot in the door. Today, however, they both gave keynote presentations. They now possessed a measure of celebrity status among the participants and therefore, the capital to approach anyone there. Now they were making rounds at the banquet hall, working their way to their marks.

Warsaw met Liam Brunner earlier that day after giving her presentation. He was an Executive VP of Crédit Suisse, the second-largest bank in Switzerland. He managed a division serving high net worth international investors. She walked up to him at the bar where he was refilling his drink and she touched his elbow. He turned and smiled. They exchanged pleasantries, and he recommended they find a quiet booth in the adjacent bar.

Warsaw sipped her Chardonnay as their conversation eventually transitioned from academic to personal. Before long, Brunner's vodka martinis began to take a toll.

"Liam," Warsaw said, leaning in. "I have to apologize to you."

The banker stared at her quizzically. "Nonsense! For what?"

"Well, you see," Warsaw continued, "I have an ulterior motive for speaking with you."

He grinned at her, his thick Swiss accent slurring now. "That's OK, Elaine, I have ulterior motives all the time. I'm a banker, after all." At that, he broke into laughter.

Warsaw laughed as well, despite loathing the man completely. He was a dirty old drunk, but it *was* funny. "This particular motive," she continued, "is very specific. I represent a group interested in your bank's engagement with a certain international organization. I need you to give me the details of that arrangement."

It took a few seconds for Brunner to process what she had said. As he responded, his countenance changed from happily relaxed to inquisitively careful. "Wait, what? You'll have to be more specific than that, darling. If you are asking me for client information, I think we both know that will never happen."

Warsaw remained stone-faced. "Actually, dear Liam, you're going to tell me everything I want to know. I am quite prepared to expose very lurid and embarrassing information about you to your family, your friends, your employer, and to the authorities. I have photos...videos too. High-resolution."

An hour later, she had what she needed. He threatened her with legal action at first, and to have her thrown out of the conference. Then he offered her money. Seeing that nothing would move her, he gave in. Warsaw had him transfer a few sensitive files to her mobile phone, and that was that.

"Pleasure doing business with you, Liam," she quipped as she walked off, leaving him with his head hung in his hands at the bar.

Singe struck out with his first target, who left the conference after the last session for a personal emergency. Fortunately, the second was there tonight. Singe observed him chatting with another attendee across the room. Robert Boddens was an executive at Cainvest Bank and Trust Limited, an institution known for its fierce protection of their clientele's privacy. Boddens would normally have been a particularly difficult target, except for the fact he had been skimming millions from his clients by shaving tiny percentages of returns off their accounts for over a decade.

Singe approached the two men, introduced himself, and inquired about the island's landmarks and attractions. They seemed irritated at first to be interrupted for such a mundane change in conversation, but soon warmed to him. They were both from the island and proudly explained the best places to see and visit to the curious American. After a while, Boddens' colleague excused himself and Singe stopped him abruptly, getting right to the point. Given the gravity of the kompromat the NSA had on him, Boddens folded quickly as well.

◆

Admiral Clausen was elated by Team Apogee's productivity. Yes, there had been a few hiccups, but as complex missions go, it had been a total success to date. In terms of intel, the New York team had been wildly successful. Not just because of the incredible cache of information they had gleaned, but because they had accomplished it without tipping anyone off. The Caribbean team had also come through. They collected significant details on the money trails and identified what could be a key player at or near the top of Typhon, Jefferey Gunderson. The Agency was running down all leads and by tomorrow, he intended to make a preliminary report to POTUS.

The update from Mac and Franklin had been equally heartening. He was relieved Joe had come through it unscathed. They lost Von Stemp but had gained a Typhon insider—Jasmine Snow.

The field operations were going well but due to its enormous complexity, strategic work was moving slowly. Ever since Clausen came to believe that the current state of the world was not a natural evolution, he had been worried there might be a point of no return.

That no matter what Apogee was able to accomplish, its demise might already be unstoppable. It was entirely plausible they could mitigate, stop, and ultimately reverse the current course if they'd begun their efforts early enough. But systemic change driven by unpredictable unnatural forces was problematic to forecast, and the inertia of it all might just be too great at this point.

The *Butterfly Effect*, seemingly insignificant events that lead to global impact. *Had they already passed the point of no return?* He just didn't know. All their efforts could be moot. It could already be over, and they wouldn't even know, until much later. Clausen straightened his back and willed himself to stop this train of thought. It was counterproductive. Gymnasts are taught *where you look, you go*. He wasn't going to waste any more time looking down.

CHAPTER TWENTY-FOUR

PARIS BLUES

After ringing off with Mac, Franklin went to work setting up a base of operations. To expedite things, he made a phone call to the Defense Attaché at the U.S. Embassy. The 'DATT' was the primary military advisor to the Ambassador and Country Team on military issues within France.

Within hours he had a sit down with the DATT who, after a few phone calls, was able to resource Franklin with one of the CIA's Paris safehouses. The three-bedroom condo was near the center of the city. It was well stocked with medical supplies, boxes of varied caliber ammunition, handguns, and extra magazines, tasers, flash bang grenades and other defensive armaments. Things were looking up.

Mac and Snow touched down later that afternoon and by the time they got to the condo, Franklin had been on and off the line with the Agency most of the day. New information was coming in from the NSA. A clearer picture of the scope and breadth of Typhon's operations was developing.

Franklin greeted his good friend warmly. Then he turned to Snow. "Ms. Snow, I presume."

Snow smiled. "Please, call me Jasmine. Can I call you Joe?"

"Sure. Welcome to the team," Franklin responded directly.

Over the next several hours, the three deliberated about how the next stages of their mission should unfold. Snow proved to be transparent and credible, readily willing to share her knowledge of Typhon's inner workings, personnel, and secrets. Before they realized, it was already 10:00 pm and they were finishing a meal of microwaved pizza and beer.

"OK team, let's recap," Mac said. "Based on our new intel, there is no longer any doubt it is an organization called 'Typhon' that is driving global disruption with the aim of creating a new world order under their control. They have been operating under the radar for many years, perhaps decades. Agency leadership is executing strategic initiatives to neutralize their resources worldwide. Our teammates in New York and The Caribbean are finishing up their missions and will head back to Stone Harbor to await further instructions. We…" Mac pointed to Franklin, Snow, and then himself, "are tasked with neutralizing Typhon's leadership and command structure. The rest of the team may join us as the plan evolves. Our immediate objective is to locate, subdue, and interrogate Wart Von Stemp, Nicholi Krishinko, and Jefferey Gunderson."

◆

Von Stemp called Nicholi Krishinko shortly after his narrow escape the night before. He was resting comfortably with his left shoulder immobilized when Krishinko arrived at the safehouse.

"Glad to see you are OK, Wart. How are you feeling?"

"Not too bad. I had surgery this morning. The pain medication is beginning to wear off." Then he smiled at Krishinko. "But I don't mind. I like to feel the pain. It reminds me of what I am going to do to that son of a bitch the next time I see him."

Krishinko nodded. "Well, the good news is that you will recover. There will be some rehab. The bad news is you probably won't be sculling any time soon."

Von Stemp frowned. "We'll see about that."

Krishinko knew better than to argue. Von Stemp was a stubborn German. "Yes, we'll see. It matters not, as long as you can continue to pull your weight." He leveled his eyes at Von Stemp now, menacingly. "But if you screw up again, I'll shoot you myself. And there will be no need for rehab."

Von Stemp said nothing for a moment, then acceded. "Ich verstehe. So, what's the plan now?"

"We'll get to that," Krishinko answered. "Jefferey is on his way here right now. We'll reconvene early with him tomorrow morning. In the meantime, I want all our global comm systems functioning at one hundred percent. We also need status reports from all regions. Print three copies—we will burn them afterwards. I'm going to call the boss and see if we have any more information on this ground team. We need to understand exactly what we're dealing with."

Krishinko left the room and sent a coded message to Peter Gunderson:

URGENT: Need details on fed assault team: who, how many, skills, etc. Must eliminate. Consider LR.

♦

Peter Gunderson had just finished his 10K morning run when he received Krishinko's message. The Russian didn't text unless it was important. Until now, Gunderson had been reluctant to activate certain strategic resources. Their exposure could jeopardize him personally. There were only a handful of these highly placed operators, and they were only to be used as part of Typhon's LAST RESORT protocol. He had to decide if Krishinko's was a legitimate LR request. He was primed to unleash the Chaos Protocol. At this point it might be illogical not to. He was beginning to feel something he hadn't felt before, however. Something that made him edgy. It was leading to stress, making it harder to sleep at night lately. Could it be, fear?

Gunderson couldn't risk being personally exposed. Typhon would fall apart without him. But at the same time, various parts of his plan were failing. It was a time for extraordinary measures. He could risk perhaps a modicum of the protocol, maybe one LR operative. And he knew exactly who that would be. From what little intel he received from Senator Billings he knew that it was an NSA team, and that could only come from the top. Admiral James Clausen. It was time to call in a big chit.

Martin Stabler was methodically reviewing incoming updates on Apogee when his mobile phone buzzed. It wasn't the normal long buzz that meant he'd just received a text message. It was two short buzzes. His heart jumped. He looked to the open door of his office, then got up and closed and locked the door and sat back down. Beads of sweat were forming on his brow. He wiped his forehead with his shirtsleeve and tapped on the calculator app. There was a '1' in the field at the top. He entered a short series of numbers and a message appeared:

Need all details on NSA team pursuing Typhon. Names, SSNs, last known locations, current mission directives. Immediately.

Stabler had hoped this day would never come, but here it was. Until now, they'd never asked him for anything. He'd nearly forgotten about it, hoping they had forgotten about him. When he made his bargain with Jefferey Gunderson, he made it very clear that he could only be used once. Chances were, the Agency would find out soon enough and he'd be gone—booted from the NSA or in jail. Either way, unusable to Typhon. So, they should wait until they really, *really* needed something from him. Jefferey had agreed, and Stabler felt comfortable that he'd end up retiring without ever being contacted. The large sum deposited into his secure Cayman Bank account was too much to pass up. Especially considering he may never have to do a thing. But here it was. And he had no choice. So, he typed a reply, acknowledging the request and that the requested information would be uploaded before the end of the day. He took a deep breath and pressed send.

There were two ways to manage the request. One was to put the data on a flash drive and transmit it later that night from his home. That approach *felt* safer—but one way or the other, it would leave a metadata trail. Only secure, approved thumb drives were allowed to be used in the building. Anything else and his system would freeze, IT would be alerted. If he used an approved drive, his name, and the actions he took, the time and date he took them, and the transferred filenames would be recorded. He'd be found out eventually unless he were somehow able to scrub the server activity log. It wasn't beyond his capability, but it wasn't something he would call his specialty, either. The other option was to pull up the files and take photos using his phone camera. Personal cell phones weren't allowed in the office—he would have to sneak it in. More time-intensive and riskier on the front end, but no red flags. No way to prove anything without accessing his phone. He went with option two.

As the Assistant to the Director, Martin had access to most sensitive files at the Agency. This included Top-Secret Cryptanalytic and Cryptologic records and files. His access was broader than anyone at the Agency, save for the Director himself, and he was briefed in to Apogee, an active and very important operation. There was nothing unusual about his accessing those files now.

Over the next two hours, Martin kept his door closed. He was interrupted a few times, once by the Admiral and twice more by administrative assistants. Each time he was able to put his phone in his desk before answering the door. When he was finished, he used an app on his phone to combine all the photos into a single PDF.

As the afternoon sun was setting, Stabler was satisfied he had captured enough detail to satisfy Gunderson. He used the Typhon fake calculator app to encrypt and securely transfer the file. He then deleted all the photos and the PDF and deleted them again from his 'deleted' folders, feeling quite confident that no one would ever find out. His confidence was quickly overcome, however, by guilt and shame, and then more so by a mounting fear that these requests of him might continue.

Peter Gunderson was becoming concerned after an hour passed and his demand of Stabler had not yet been met. By the end of the second hour, he found himself uncharacteristically pacing in his office as his anger and trepidation grew. He was not used to incompetence or delays, and his patience was wearing thin.

Suddenly, the female voice of his computer announced, "Incoming file from Martin Stabler."

"Display it," Gunderson commanded urgently as he stepped over to his console. On his screen was a picture of a page titled *Apogee Overview*. That file was three pages long. He scrolled through quickly— the PDF was made up of nearly 200 photographs. There was a file titled *Team Apogee* and others titled *Set 1, Set 2, Set 3, M Initiative, m Initiative, NSC Logistics,* and *NATCOG.*

Those were just the first nine folders. There were others. Gunderson was stunned at the breadth of it all, and elated that Stabler proved to be, in a single stroke, the most valuable asset he'd ever bought, well worth the $350,000 he'd given him. Gunderson wondered if he should have pushed this button earlier, but quickly dismissed the thought. Stabler could finger him in an instant if he were caught. But Stabler had a wife and three children. Gunderson had mentioned their names after concluding the original deal. Even if he were caught, he doubted Stabler would put them in harm's way. But one never knows...

Four hours of uninterrupted reading later, Gunderson leaned back in the big leather chair. Stabler's report was a comprehensive roadmap of Apogee's operations and plans. For the first time, Gunderson felt like he was back in control. He now held a huge advantage. Even though his adversaries apparently knew a fair amount about Typhon, Gunderson now knew everything that they knew. Which means he also knew what they *didn't* know and could modify his strategies appropriately to take advantage of that.

He would need to abandon his current headquarters in Bryn Mawr, Pennsylvania and relocate to his backup in Auckland, New Zealand. He would fake his death and hoped that it would be convincing enough to work.

Every resource and capability that existed here, existed as well at the mountain retreat down under he'd purchased via a shell company a decade earlier. He would set the house to self-destruct, and his DNA would conveniently be found among the wreckage. A precisely orchestrated natural gas fire would thoroughly incinerate everything. While he wistfully regretted losing the estate, he reminded himself it was just another expense, another tool to use. When the tool outlived its usefulness, it was discarded for another. By the time the last smoldering remains were squelched by the Main Line's fire trucks, Gunderson would be relaxing on his 500-acre ranch 7,200 miles away, drinking a glass of twenty-year-old scotch and enjoying the beautiful mountain view.

CHAPTER TWENTY-FIVE

STACKED DECK

The next morning, Mac and his Paris team checked in with Clausen to see if there were any new leads on Typhon's leaders' whereabouts. The news was not heartening. Though the Agency was engaged in a massive data search, they did not have any marching orders for Team Apogee. Mac found it almost unbelievable that with the computing power and information at their disposal that they were unable to move quickly on a few high-profile individuals. The truth was, the Admiral wanted to make sure there were no mistakes. He was already dealing with the FAA, FBI, and local police agencies trying to smooth over and cover up some of the collateral damage they'd already left behind.

The three were drinking coffee quietly in the kitchen. Snow broke the silence. "Let's go over everything we know again and see if anything breaks loose."

"Ok," Mac agreed hesitantly. "But until we get anything new, this is the last time. I don't know about you, but I'm beginning to get tired of waiting and reviewing." He sipped from his cup, both hands on the warm mug. "Von Stemp. He probably would have needed medical attention, but he didn't check into a hospital, as far as we can tell. Not within a hundred kilometers of Paris, anyway. He would have used a fake name, but a gunshot wound would be reported to the police. With medical attention, it's likely he was fit for travel. He could be anywhere by now. It could be he was treated by a private doctor and is laying low at a safehouse nearby, not unlike this one." "Nevertheless," Mac went on, "if he got that treatment at the safe house, it must not be too far away. Anything else come to mind?"

Both Franklin and Snow shook their heads.

"OK. Jasmine, tell us everything you know about Typhon and their operations that might help us to locate Von Stemp."

Snow's exposure to Typhon leadership had been limited to Von Stemp and Krishinko. She knew from her interactions that neither of them was at the apex of the organization. They all knew that now; from the intel they'd obtained. Peter and Jefferey Gunderson were likely the top bosses. Unfortunately, that information was of little value in helping them locate any of them in France. However, she did know Typhon had safe houses. In fact, she said, there were three in the UK, and she had their addresses.

"What the hell, Jasmine!" Mac exclaimed. "That's information you should have given me right up front. Why am I just hearing about this now?"

She looked flustered. "You're right, I'm sorry. But it's not as if we've had time yet to do a proper debrief. I've been giving you everything you've asked for and offering what I think might be helpful. That's what I'm doing now."

Mac realized she was right—there had been no time. And she had been totally transparent so far.

Franklin stepped in, a pen in his hand. "What are the addresses? Are there any commonalities between the three that might allow us to narrow the search here?"

"We need to send the addresses over to headquarters immediately," Mac interjected.

"Of course. Well, let's see," said Snow. "Now that you mention it, all three of the UK safe houses were in rural areas outside of London. They were all secluded, and all three had at least three bedrooms."

"How much acreage?" Mac asked.

"At least ten acres give or take," she answered.

"Anything else unique about them," Mac pressed.

"Not really." Then she paused, scrunching up her face. "No fences or gates, no obnoxiously obvious security systems… Wait, there *was* something. All three had at least one outbuilding big enough to house large equipment. They also all had very specialized, mobile exterior lighting systems. They would store those in the buildings. I was never told what they were for. I only happened to see them set up one day in the back yard during an orientation visit. They didn't tell me everything, mind you. But it was the kind of lighting you might see at a high school rugby match or something."

"Was there a field on each of the properties? Flat, somewhat large? Was the grass cut low?"

"Yes, why?" Snow responded.

"Huh," Mac pondered.

"What?" prodded Franklin.

"My guess is that there aren't that many properties in and around Paris that have helicopters coming and going."

Snow and Franklin looked at each other, then back to Mac.

"Let's get the Agency on the horn and see if they can't use some of that computing power to narrow our search based on private chopper traffic around Paris."

♦

Jefferey Gunderson arrived at the safehouse a little later than he anticipated due to a weather delay out of Philadelphia. His helicopter was fueled and waiting on the pad beside Typhon's private hanger. Normally, he would have driven but the safehouse was in a rural area on the other side of Paris. Traffic was terrible, and time was wasting. Besides, there were too many traffic cameras between the airport and his destination. He couldn't risk being located in Paris. Or anywhere, for that matter.

After the short flight, he disembarked from under the whooping rotor blades and slow jogged to the one-story stone structure. Krishinko stood in the arched doorway to greet him and ushered him inside as the pilot drove a Kubota 4x4 with a hitch to the helicopter. It would be towed into the adjacent outbuilding to avoid prying eyes.

Jefferey wasted no time demanding an update as the two men sat down in the modest living room. "What's going on with Wart? Jefferey asked.

"His shoulder is pretty messed up," Krishinko answered. "Besides that, he's fine."

"Why isn't he here?" Gunderson looked irritated.

He's resting. I guess he didn't hear the helo. Should I get him?"

"Not yet. What is your assessment? Is he a liability?"

Krishinko needed to be careful how he answered this question, otherwise Von Stemp might not live out the day. "I wouldn't be sending him into combat anytime soon. But Wart is not like most guys."

"What do you mean?"

Krishinko continued. "He is one hundred percent committed. Loyal. He is incredibly fit and strong as a bull. He can withstand high levels of pain; he's not even taking meds right now. Bottom line, if we need him, even with a bad arm, he's still better than almost anyone else. Plus, there's a lot he can do that doesn't require both arms—communications, logistics. He's very capable."

Gunderson took a moment to respond. He knew Krishinko and Von Stemp went back a long way. That could be affecting Krishinko's judgment. If Von Stemp was a liability, he had to be removed from play, and Gunderson knew they couldn't take the chance that he might be captured alive. He knew too much.

Krishinko could see the wheels turning. "Two other points. We could use his help taking these guys down. Von Stemp is the best sniper we have, and he can still do that. Listen, I know you think I'm biased when it comes to him, and maybe I am, but I don't let that cloud my judgement or get in the way. I told him that if he screwed up again, I would shoot him myself. He knows I was not kidding."

Gunderson nodded slowly. "OK, I'll go along with it, but understand—the second he can't pull his weight, or if he jeopardizes our mission in any way, I expect you to pull the trigger. Do we have an understanding?"

Krishinko acknowledged seriously, careful not to let out a sigh of relief. "I understand, Jeffery. You have my word."

Gunderson stood up from his chair and went to the kitchen. "You got some coffee on?" he yelled.

"Yes," answered Krishinko, "on the counter."

"Thanks. Now go wake him up. We need to go over our new plans."

By the time he returned to the living room, Krishinko and Von Stemp were seated at the rustic coffee table in front of a large limestone fireplace, a stack of dry oak logs stacked on the grate. Gunderson placed three cups of steaming black coffee on the table.

"Good morning, Wart. Sorry about your mishap and I hope you're up to this."

"Thanks Jefferey, good to see you. And don't worry, I am more than ready." Von Stemp answered back.

"I'm counting on it," Jefferey said, smiling. Then he clapped his hands. "Ok, let's get to it. My father sent me here with one mission, to take out this NSA black ops team. It is the most important thing on our plate. If we fail, Typhon fails and sooner or later, we'll all end up dead or in jail. And we have just seventy-two hours to do it. If we don't succeed within that timeframe, he is going to pull the trigger on the Chaos Protocol. It was always planned as a last resort, if there was some critical threat. But we'd rather not do it, of course. Chaos has an important purpose, mind you. It will allow us to succeed while at the same time, stovepiping and granularizing the organization worldwide. It breaks all the connections. Communications stop, all data and records are destroyed, everywhere, all at once. But of course, we will lose control. Our entire plan, everything we've worked towards and built over the course of decades will be trapped in an unmanageable and less predictable state. We must succeed in eliminating this team, and quickly." Gunderson then booted his laptop and began reviewing the report from his father while Von Stemp and Krishinko looked on.

After thirty minutes, Jefferey again opened the conversation. "It looks like this is just a small part of what we were able to get from the NSA. It was a treasure trove. But this is better—it's everything we need, and nothing that we don't. It is also important to know that they've identified all of us, including me and my father. Life as we've known it is over, for now. There may come a time when we can reemerge, after the new world order has been stabilized, but for now, we are some of the most wanted men on the face of the Earth. My father is relocating our headquarters as we sit here."

"We have the names, profiles, and recent locations of each member of the Apogee team, including those here in Paris. Since this report is only a few hours old, we can assume that Mac Sisco has arrived, or will arrive soon here in Paris. The most unsettling news is," he looked straight at Krishinko menacingly. "Your girl Jasmine Snow from the UK had contact with one of the NSA agents, Mac Sisco. Do we know what happened? Do they have her?"

Von Stemp interceded. "I'm aware. She alerted me ahead of their meeting and asked me for advice. I told her to interrogate him and then to terminate him. She hasn't reported back yet, I've been kind of busy, as you know," he pointed to his shoulder. "I haven't followed up yet. In any case, Nicholi and I both recruited her. She was the perfect convert; she met all the criteria. She's done an exemplary job for us so far, and she has skeletons. I wouldn't worry about Snow."

"Too good to be true usually is," Jefferey countered. We have no way of knowing whose side she is on. If she attempts contact with us, which they would want her to do, we'll have to be very careful. For now, we must tread lightly."

That decision behind them, Jefferey continued to layout his plan. "Right now, we have a stacked deck. We know everything about them, and we know everything they know about us up to a few hours ago. And they don't know we know these things. We could launch an attack in an hour and catch them completely by surprise, but that would be hasty, I think. There are still things we don't know. We don't know how fortified their safehouse is, the security outlay, what weapons they have, if they have backup resources. And we don't have time to do proper reconnaissance to figure all that out." We need *them* to come to *us*."

He went on. "We need them to think *they* have the advantage, that *they* will catch *us* by surprise. Nicholi, tell our pilot to take the car back to Paris and to standby. If we have to get out of here fast, you can fly us out."

"Right," Krishinko replied. "But they don't know where this safehouse is. How are we going to tip them off without exposing our knowledge of them?"

Gunderson smiled. "That's not as tricky as it sounds. Wart, tell Snow to fly down and meet us here immediately. We need whatever information she might have on Sisco, and we could use her skillset when the NSA team rolls in. Once she gets here, I'll have her message Sisco. She has his number. She can tell him she changed her mind and wants to defect, or whatever. That she's hiding out here, alone and afraid, and doesn't want any trouble. She will *give him* our address. If she pushes back or doesn't respond, we can assume they've turned her."

Both Krishinko and Von Stemp nodded their approval of the plan.

◆

The walls of the team's safehouse were pinned with topographical maps of the French countryside, aerial photos, and printouts of commercial and private helicopter schedules.

"My eyes are beginning to blur," complained the big Seal as he tacked on another document.

"The search area is still too large," Mac lamented as he scanned the walls. "We're running out of time. Meanwhile, Typhon is moving on, moving forward, going to ground, who knows. They may be looking for us right here in Paris. Meanwhile, we're just sitting ducks with no backup."

Jasmine yelled suddenly. "Bloody hell!"

The others looked up expectantly.

"What?" Mac demanded.

"You're not going to believe this. "I just got a message from Von Stemp." She showed them her phone.

Am with NK at SH1—Coulommiers, Chessy off A4 motorway. FRANCE. Limited connectivity. Fly down here and meet us ASAP. —VS

"We are in business!" she exclaimed, grinning.

"How about that shit," said Franklin. "A break at last."

"Talk about good timing," Mac agreed. "Honestly, I almost can't believe it. Let's find this place on a map."

It was a large farm. The main house was L-shaped, typical of the Brie region, surrounded by fifteen acres of gently sloping pastureland and greenbelt.

Mac studied the map. "Joe, contact headquarters and see if we can get a satellite over the property. We need some hi-res closeups of the residence and outbuildings. It doesn't look like there will be much cover going in. While we wait for that, let's break this down some more. What's our approach, how will we engage and exfil. What are our contingencies, the major risks."

He continued. "The obvious plan is a standard a team assault, around three am. We could also decide to let Jasmine do what they instructed her to do—go in ahead of us. She could report back to us, give us the intel from inside. Maybe even distract them or mitigate their response."

Franklin scowled. "No offense, Jasmine, but Mac—she hasn't earned that level of trust. I'm not sure she ever could. You just asked about the major risks—she's certainly one of them."

Snow looked away as Mac held up his hands in a cautionary manner. "Joe, you're right. It's just an option. I'm not saying it's the best one, only that it is one on to consider."

Up to now Snow had been quiet, but now she spoke confidently. "Well, if I get a vote, I vote for option two."

"How do you feel about direct engagement with these guys?" Mac asked candidly. "You know them. Do *they* have your trust? Would they let their guard down around you?"

Snow responded, "I don't think they really trust anyone. Having me on board was a necessity. It is a strategic role. If not me, it would have been someone else. I've done this kind of fieldwork before, many times. I can handle myself."

"Jasmine," asked Mac, "you said you contacted Von Stemp in advance of our first meeting. He knows I'm on to you. What was his reply?"

She remained stoic, but her face was flushed. "He said…*interrogate, terminate and report back*. It was via a text. I have yet to respond."

Mac sighed. "Well, this could be a problem. It's only been a couple days, but he would have expected an answer. I'm guessing his little scuffle with Joe here, getting shot, and being on the run has kept him otherwise engaged, but I guarantee he's thinking about it now. They want to interrogate you. If we send you in, it would be with the knowledge that they might know or suspect you have been turned. You would have to convince them that you haven't. Reply to him. Let him know you will catch the next flight and be there soon. Tell him that you tried to kill me, but I escaped. You followed but lost me. Tell him you think I will come back for you. Make it sound like you're afraid."

"I can do that," she replied confidently, her complexion returning to normal.

"I'm inclined to send Jasmine in, Joe," said Mac. "Having someone on the inside is just too valuable. Our chances for success would go up dramatically, you know that. Them knowing she had contact with me is a problem, but maybe we can use it to our advantage."

Franklin grunted concession, though it was clear he did not agree with it.

They couldn't be sure that there weren't others with Krishinko and Von Stemp at the property. They also didn't know how injured Von Stemp was, whether he would be able to help put up a defense. They had to assume he would be in play. Striking with precision and speed would be critical. After reviewing additional photos sent from Fort Meade, the three worked for two more hours on the details before being satisfied that they had a solid plan. All that was left was execution.

CHAPTER TWENTY-SIX

SURPRISE SURPRISE

It was almost 2:00 am when they pulled the rental over, less than a kilometer from the entrance to the property. Mac and Franklin exited the vehicle and quickly disappeared into the dark. After thirty minutes, they arrived at a copse of trees near the edge of a broad pasture. Several outbuildings stood to the sides and back of the main residence. Numerous floodlights illuminated the house. Not enough to look strange, but enough to make ingress more difficult. A lone front window was lit from the inside of the house. So far, they hadn't noticed any security cameras, motion detectors, or other security tech.

Mac spoke into his earpiece. "In position. Cleared in."

"Copy," Snow replied.

Mac's voice was almost a whisper. "Joe and I will give you fifteen minutes. That should be enough time for you to sit down with them and begin debriefing. Don't forget about the door."

"Copy," she came back again.

Twenty seconds later, they watched as Jasmine drove up to the house, parked, and knocked on the door. Almost immediately, a second window lit up. A few moments went by, and someone let her inside.

"We'll go in fast and low, first to the barn, there." He pointed. "Then to the front door. You go first, I'll follow. A straight run, it will be less visible. Less exposure."

Franklin gave him a thumbs-up and they waited. A second house window lit up.

Mac looked at his watch. "Move."

Silently, they accelerated into a crouching sprint toward the barn.

Jasmine put her earpiece in the glove box, got out of the car, and walked the fieldstone path to the door and knocked. After a minute, the door opened, revealing both Von Stemp and Krishinko. Von Stemp's shoulder and upper arm was bandaged and in a sling. He held his Sig lowered, in his good hand.

"Hello Jasmine," Von Stemp greeted her. "Let's go to the living room and talk. Do you need anything?"

"I'm good, thanks," she replied, and followed them into the living room, leaving the door unlocked behind her.

Krishinko turned on the light and they sat.

"Jasmine," Von Stemp said dramatically. "I'm glad you could make it."

She kept her voice steady and confident. "I came as fast as I could."

"You made good time. You remember Nicholi, yes?"

"Yes," she responded. "Good evening, Nicholi."

Krishinko acknowledged her with a nod. "We have a lot to discuss. Before we start, Wart—frisk her, please."

Snow objected dramatically. "Seriously? I thought we were past all this. We've been working together a long time now."

"Have we?" questioned Krishinko. "We can't be too careful, can we Jasmine?"

Before Von Stemp could even get up, Snow handed him her concealed handgun.

"Any other little surprises?" queried Krishinko.

"It was hard enough to get a weapon into France," Snow shot back, irritated. "We're all armed, Nicholi. I carry for my day job, and the work I do with you is no less dangerous, if not more so. I could have been killed yesterday," she stated flatly, glaring at Von Stemp.

They both seemed to accept it. Von Stemp then began questioning her about the details of her interaction with Sisco.

Outside, Mac and Franklin were ready to make their move.

"Go try the door," Mac whispered. "I'll cover you. If it's unlocked, give me a thumbs-up. Thumbs down otherwise. I'd rather try the back entry before breaking down the door.

"Roger that," replied Franklin. Then he took off.

No sooner did Franklin touch the handle when he heard a voice off to the side. "Don't move, Mr. Franklin, or you die."

Franklin froze. From the corner of his eye, he saw a shadowy form emerge from a tall bush against the house, head covered by a black balaclava.

"Now, open the door and step inside," the man continued.

Franklin didn't recognize the voice. He knew Mac was seeing it all and was ready for the shit to hit the fan. He did as he was told and entered the house. His captor silently followed a few feet behind him and closed the door once he was clear.

"Very good, Mr. Franklin." He waved the gun to the left. "Now, go to the living room."

Again, Franklin did as he was told and walked into the room. Wart Von Stemp, Snow, and a man he recognized as Nicholi Krishinko were all seated.

"Nicholi," the man commanded, "search our new guest, then zip tie his hands."

Krishinko smirked. "My pleasure."

"*You again,*" Von Stemp intoned venomously.

The man removed his balaclava and sat next to Von Stemp, still holding the handgun.

Disarmed and subdued, Franklin was pushed by Krishinko into a chair next to Snow and across from his captors. He was careful to show no recognition of Krishinko or the third man, who he now recognized as Jefferey Gunderson.

Gunderson glared at Von Stemp. "You're an idiot. He followed you here." Then he turned to Franklin. "Who else came with you? Who knows you are here?"

Franklin didn't answer. Gunderson stood up, moved his handgun to his left hand and approached the big Seal. Without warning, he brutally stuck him squarely in the face with his right fist, sending his head whipping backwards sharply and his upper body slamming back into the chair.

Blood spurted from below his eye and his vision blurred.

Gunderson knelt, his face inches from Franklin's. In a slow growl he demanded, "who else knows you're here?"

Franklin stared straight into his eyes, then smashed his forehead down into the man's nose, audibly snapping the cartilage. Gunderson was sent careening backwards and onto the floor.

As Snow looked on, eyes wide, Krishinko and Von Stemp leapt to their feet. Franklin smiled broadly; his gleaming white teeth contrasted starkly against his bloodied face.

Gunderson was incensed. Krishinko helped him to his feet, his nose bent grotesquely to the side. More pressing, he'd been embarrassed by Franklin. He wanted badly to just shoot him, but his instincts told him that would be a mistake. They needed to know what he knew. He wouldn't break easily. It would take time and resources he didn't currently have. He wiped his face with the sleeve of his shirt, then grabbed the end of his crooked nose and jerked it back in place, grimacing. Krishinko was moving forward ready to pistol-whip their prisoner.

"Nicholi, hold your temper," he chastised. "I have plans for Mr. Franklin. Everyone just sit tight while I clean myself up." Then he left the room.

Mac witnessed Franklin's capture, cursing under his breath. He aimed and put pressure on the trigger, but then held off. He might miss, and he was at least fifty feet away. Franklin would be shot immediately. As soon as they went inside, he ran up and put his ear to the door. He could hear them walking towards the adjacent room. He positioned himself just outside the window and listened intently.

Mac gritted his teeth as he heard Gunderson hit his friend. Some muffled talking, then quiet. Mac crouched under the window. Using a small, long-handled mirror, he watched as Gunderson returned to the room. There was bluish swelling below each of his eyes, but he looked to be back in control.

Gunderson stopped in the middle of the room with his hands on his hips. "I think this has worked out quite well. We have captured a valuable enemy asset, a member of the Apogee Team. He will provide us with crucial intel and maybe even leverage against the others."

"I say we kill him," Krishinko countered. "We don't have the time or the resources to interrogate and babysit. And we can't stay here, we must assume his team knows where he is."

"I agree, let's kill this piece of garbage," Von Stemp said menacingly.

Gunderson raised his voice. "We're taking him with us, understood? With the information he has, we might be able to quickly neutralize their whole operation. Remember, timing is critical with Chaos in play," he added. Without him, we had very little chance of pulling this off. With him, it's a possibility. We're leaving right now. Wart and Jasmine, head outside. I'll have someone return your rental. Nicholi, go pull the chopper out and fire it up. I'll escort Mr. Franklin."

Mac watched and heard everything. He ran back to the barn and hid as Krishinko, Von Stemp, and Snow came out the front door. Moments later, he heard the Kubota fire up and watched it pull the helo out of the building. Krishinko jumped out and unhitched, drove it back to the barn, and closed it up. At that moment, Gunderson emerged with Franklin in front, a barrel to his back. The chopper whined and the blades began to spin. Von Stemp was directing Snow into the rear of the bird.

Mac had hoped Snow would make a move before now. Things hadn't evolved as planned, but surely she knew this was their best opportunity? He experienced a twinge of concern. Had he been wrong about her all along? Had she played them?

Gunderson and Franklin were halfway to the chopper. Mac had to make his move. He stepped out from the corner of the building, twenty feet away in a shooting stance, his P226 aimed firmly at Gunderson. Before they could notice him, he pulled the trigger, but missed. Even with the rotor noise, Gunderson heard the report and immediately turned. Krishinko was walking with his back to Mac and didn't notice. Von Stemp and Snow were still inside the helicopter.

Franklin knew exactly what was going on, however, and dove into a forward roll back up on his feet. Gunderson was caught indecisive, shoot Mac, or get his gun back on Franklin? Mac sprinted forward, attempting to sight in again on Gunderson. Just then, the engine whine increased dramatically, sending up a huge cloud of dust. Mac covered his eyes and tried to see, catching a glimpse of a stooped figure near the middle of the swirl.

Mac retreated cursing himself. As he reached the perimeter of the billowing cloud, he slammed into someone else, and they both fell to the ground. The 9mm still in his hand, Mac raised it defensively, hoping it was Gunderson.

"Hey, it's me, Joe." he heard Franklin exclaim.

All they could do at that point was to sit and watch as Gunderson's helicopter spurted up out of the top of the dust cloud, like a dragonfly off a mushroom. The helo then gained altitude and disappeared southward into the moonless sky.

CHAPTER TWENTY-SEVEN

CHANGE OF VENUE

Peter Gunderson had always been prepared for a quick exit from Philadelphia. It took less than three hours. His spies were on the lookout for any government vehicles—he knew they could be inbound to snatch him up at any moment.

If it was paper, it was burned. All computer data, files, and drives were wiped and destroyed. The fire would probably have done the trick, but Gunderson was thorough to a fault. Nothing would be found. As he drove off, he turned back for one last look at his home of so many years. Then he settled into the back seat of his limousine, a bag with two bottles of twenty-year-old scotch beside him.

The flight took just over eighteen hours, almost 9,000 miles, and he had been out of contact with Jefferey since leaving. Trusted associates at the new Typhon headquarters were prepared for his arrival, but only he could login and boot the systems. Only then could their secure networks and communications come back online. The 72-hour window was closing fast. He was bitterly upset but accepting of the fact he'd have to, more than likely, launch the Chaos Protocol.

HQ 2 was a very different than the traditional stone mansion and complex in mainline Bryn Mawr. He decided years before to establish a second headquarters as a contingency, a decision now proved fortuitous in so many ways. These days, it was illegal for anyone but citizens of New Zealand to purchase land there. It was a remote country with large tracts of rural land protected by mountainous terrain, providing unparalleled privacy. He could have built elsewhere, in Africa or South America. But New Zealand was a first-world nation, ensuring ready access to the resources and technology Typhon needed to operate. The property was situated about an hour's drive from the city, fifteen minutes by helicopter.

At over 500 acres, Ardyh Ranch was expansive. The topography was mixed, dotted with fields, and rolling hills with swaths of ancient Podocarp Forest and native bush. The main residence sat on an elevated plateau with panoramic views of the Brunderwyn Ranges and the pristine beaches and surrounding islands of the Mangawhai coast. Gunderson designed the 25,000 square foot house to be open and airy with all the requisite functional spaces to properly accommodate Typhon's complex operations. Like many of Auckland's luxury residences, it was constructed of local stone and hardwoods and furnished with rustic charm and comfort.

Detached buildings were conveniently located near the residence. One housed a gym, another served as a garage for the all-terrain vehicles, dirt bikes, and farm equipment used to maintain the estate. A modest hanger sat adjacent to a paved helipad.

As he stretched his tired muscles, Gunderson gazed out through the floor to ceiling Venetian blinds hung along the entirety of one office wall. With a sigh, he sat down at his Kohekohe wood desk and set to work. He logged in to the computer and scanned his emails and messages. Immediately, a red blinking notification informed him of an urgent message:

Engaged Apogee at SH1 Paris, recovered JS, Apogee team still operational, VTC ASAP

Gunderson could feel his blood pressure rising. His team had never failed before in an attempt to carry out an operation. Yes, this was no ordinary op. There were glitches and injuries, even losses, but these things were to be expected. Forecasted. Prepared for and mitigated. He glanced at the time on his computer. Less than twenty-four hours before he would have to launch Chaos.

He looked back to the screen and began to speak. "Computer, send an encrypted message to Jefferey."

"Yes, Mr. Gunderson. Please dictate your message," it responded.

"Jefferey, VTC at 6:00 pm New Zealand time, confirm."

The computer repeated the message and displayed it on Gunderson's flat panel. "Shall I send the message, Mr. Gunderson?"

"Yes."

Then he opened a browser and typed in a search for news of his untimely death. A local Pennsylvania news site confirmed his ruse had been a success. The Philadelphia Inquirer headline read:

INVESTMENT BANKER DIES IN CATASTROPHIC NATURAL GAS EXPLOSION AT HOME IN BRYN MAWR

Some good news, at last. He logged out and headed to the master suite for a few hours of rest before his call with Jefferey.

♦

As they flew over Paris, Jefferey Gunderson was groaning with pain. Snow was attempting to staunch the bleeding from his right calf. The round from Mac's gun barely clipped him, but it still hurt like hell. He grimaced at the pain, and with the knowledge they had failed.

He was still concerned about Snow. He could solve the problem right now. An open door, a little push... But she had come immediately, and came willingly with them. She didn't try to break off during the fight at the safehouse. It was possible, in fact very likely, that Sisco had had her under surveillance since London, and he and Franklin had simply tailed her there. But if she was now working for the NSA, her information could be vital to crushing Apogee.

Snow broke his train of thought. "Ok Jefferey, I think I've got the bleeding stopped, how does it feel?"

"How do you think it feels?" he snapped back.

"You're very lucky, actually," she responded. "It's just a surface wound."

"Well, that's encouraging, but I'm not feeling very lucky right now," he rasped.

◆

"Shit Mac, they got Jasmine," Franklin yelled as the chopper soared out of sight.

"Yeah, I know. She didn't put up much of a fight, did she? She did nothing. As if she were playing us all along. But before we panic, let's get those zip ties off your wrists."

Mac used his tactical knife to cut the ties and pulled his friend to a sitting position. "You are a sight for sore eyes," he snickered. "But you'll live."

"You betcha," Franklin responded, grinning through the blood.

They got to their feet and scanned their surroundings.

"Let's make sure there aren't any more bad guys hanging around," said Mac. "Then we can see if they left any goodies behind. I'll search the house; you take the rest. Meet me in the house when you're done."

Mac turned the house upside-down and found nothing. He sat down in the living room to contact Fort Meade when he heard Franklin coming in the front door.

"Anything?" Mac asked as he walked in.

"Nothing," Franklin responded. "I don't think they've used this safehouse very often."

"I was thinking the same thing," agreed Mac. "It's as if they knew we were coming."

Franklin sat down beside him. "You know, when Gunderson came back in the room, he mentioned Apogee. They know about us. We have a leak."

"Shit," answered Mac. "Jasmine. Damn it, I really wanted to be right about her. It's also possible Typhon has a mole at headquarters. Either way, we have a big problem."

"This is getting complicated," said Franklin.

"Getting?" Mac laughed. "You know, I can count on one hand who I can trust. POTUS, Clausen, and you and the other members of our team. That's it."

"One other thing," said Franklin. "Gunderson said 'timing is critical with Chaos in play.' What the hell is *Chaos*?"

CHAPTER TWENTY-EIGHT

REGROUP

Snow took the keys with her on the helicopter. Fortunately, Franklin was able to hotwire the rental. On the drive back, Mac fired up his secure sat phone and called Clausen.

After two rings, he answered, "Clausen."

"Admiral, this is Mac. We have a problem."

"Shoot," he replied.

Mac briefed him on the details.

Clausen seemed unsurprised. "Shit happens. You did your best. On our end, POTUS and the NSC continue to make progress, but it's slow. We had a SWAT team three miles from Gunderson's house when it exploded and burned down. Gas leak. I think that's a little convenient myself, but they say his remains were found inside. So, there's that.

"What?" Mac said stunned. "I agree. *Too* convenient."

"At this point, if he is dead, I don't know if it's good, or if it's bad."

"I don't believe in coincidences, sir. Furthermore, it adds credence to my theory that there is a mole at the Agency."

There was a long pause as Clausen considered the allegation. "As much as I hate to admit it, I agree. That is a possibility. But the jury is still out on Ms. Snow. Is there a chance one of you told her about the op to get Gunderson?"

"I wasn't briefed on it, sir. But they do know about Team Apogee, and that we are hunting them. It could be that's all it was. Bad timing for us."

"Admiral, I need some help. I planted a bug on Snow before the op. We didn't trust her then, and I still don't. But it could lead us to Jefferey Gunderson, Krishinko, and Von Stemp since she left with them. The problem is, it's super small and the range is only about a half mile with the standard receiver. I need something much more sensitive to extend the range and pick up the signal. If she's still in Paris, we might get lucky and find them."

"Well, that was a good call, Agent Sisco. I'm sure we have something that can do the trick. In fact, Paris Station probably has something. I'll call the station chief and get back with you."

"Thank you, sir. I'm betting that Jefferey and company will be meeting soon with other Typhon leadership. Perhaps even with his allegedly deceased dad. That's something we'd love to listen in on before taking them down."

"Maybe so," said the Admiral. "Listen, since you don't yet know where they are headed, you should probably return to the safehouse and wait for my call on the receiver. And I'll have someone start combing our servers for any evidence of a leak. The rest of your team is on call to join you, either there in Paris, or elsewhere, as needed. I'm going to brief President Holbrook in the morning."

With that, the two men terminated the call.

"I got most of that," commented Franklin as they drove along the Seine. "Now I see why you didn't freak out about losing Jasmine.

When did you plant the bug?"

"It was a last-minute thing, just in case. I put it in her bag when we were back in London," Mac replied.

Franklin nodded. "OK. But what do you think about her? Is she on our side, or theirs?"

"I don't know," Mac responded. "Maybe both. She has a history of taking whichever side suits her at the time."

"If so, she's playing a dangerous game. It means her chances of being taken out are doubled."

"Maybe," Mac replied. "I'd like to think, however, that she's on our side. If she is, then it makes our job so much easier. That would also mean we're going to have to rescue her, Joe."

CHAPTER TWENTY-NINE

THE CHASE

Peter Gunderson's death shook financial sectors across the globe. Markets immediately experienced precipitous drops. Mac's concern regarding an Agency infiltration prompted Clausen to mount an immediate forensic investigation of the remains of Gunderson's residence and a deep dive into his personal history. His team reported back quickly with the results.

There was no evidence Gunderson faked his death. Every indication was that he perished in the fire. He owned several additional residences in the U.S. and two in Europe, but he hadn't been to any of them in the past three months. None of his registered aircraft had filed a flight plan, and his yacht *Prosperity* floated empty in its Chesapeake Bay slip. Finally, his DNA was found in the vicinity of the master suite.

While not overwhelming, the evidence pointing to Gunderson's death was convincing. But it did not mean the mission was over. The organization was vast, and he probably had a succession plan for his son in place. He needed to investigate the mole issue, and the rest of Typhon still had to be dismantled. Thanks to Mac's foresight and the Agency's technical expertise, they would be soon tracking Jasmine Snow hopefully, the location of Jefferey Gunderson, Krishinko, and Von Stemp.

Back in the Paris safehouse, Mac and Franklin were getting restless.

"This sucks," lamented the big Seal as he paced across the room.

Mac agreed. Time was not on their side. "I feel your pain, Joe. But all we can do is wait right now."

"On the bright side," Mac responded, "Soon, we should know exactly where they are." Again, Franklin nodded and said, "I guess you're right, so why don't I feel good about this?"

It was then that Mac's mobile buzzed. The familiar gravelly voice of the Admiral came on the line.

"Mac, I just got an update from my boys downstairs. First, we completed our investigation into Gunderson's death and can now say, with a high degree of certainty, that he died in the fire. As for the potential leak, I don't have anything yet. I'm working on it."

"Great news, Admiral. His death should disrupt the organization. They may overreact, do something impulsive. And we'll notice."

"Second, a CIA officer should be dropping off the receiver you need at any moment. His name is Martin. He'll knock four times, keep an ear out."

"More good news, thanks Admiral."

"Keep up the good work and let me know as soon as you have them."

"Will do. Take care sir."

The line went dead.

Almost immediately, there was a knock at the door, four times in succession. Mac looked through the peephole and opened the door.

Martin didn't bother to ask to come in, instead handing Mac the case. "It's mobile, with a satellite uplink. It's already configured, just turn it on. It will allow you to locate your tracker anywhere in the world unless it's in a dead spot. We have good coverage, but we can't see everywhere. Your tracker has a battery life of around a week. After that, you're dead in the water. When you're done with it, call us and we'll come pick it up. Good luck." He held out a business card with nothing but a phone number on it.

"Thanks," Mac said, taking the card and shaking his hand. Then Martin promptly turned and walked away.

Mac closed the door. "That guy has the personality of a brick."

Franklin chuckled. "Who cares. We have what we need now. Let's boot it up."

Mac placed the case on the kitchen table and opened it. He quickly located the power button and turned it on. The screen came alive, showing a map of the world. After about thirty seconds, a blinking yellow dot appeared, alongside a data box showing latitude, longitude, elevation, vector, and velocity. Both leaned forward in unison.

"Shit, she's on a jet," remarked Franklin. "Moving over 500 miles per hour. Off the southern tip of India. Looks like their headed to Australia."

Mac immediately called Clausen back on speakerphone to tell him the news.

The Admiral was elated. "Well guys, it sounds like you need to prep for a rapid deployment. I'll let the rest of the team know to do the same. Text me the flight information off the receiver—we'll look for a flight plan and see if they are on radar. We might even be able to pick them up on satellite. Wherever they land, that's where you'll all be going. Let's keep each other in the loop."

Both Apogee agents were silent in thought for a moment after the Admiral rang off.

Franklin broke the silence. "I'm going to pack my duffle, heat some pizza, drink a Guinness and try to get some shut eye."

Mac nodded in agreement. "Sounds like a good plan. I'm in."

◆

The Gulfstream G650 was among the fastest long-haul private jets in the world. They required only one refuel to complete the 11,700-mile flight. If Jefferey could have paced the length of the cabin, he would have, but his injured foot limited his mobility. They had been in the air for hours and Von Stemp, Krishinko and Snow were dozing. The turbulence was getting worrisome as the big plane attempted to navigate around several lines of thunderstorms. A chiming accompanied by seatbelts told them it wasn't over yet. Jefferey tightened his belt and peered out the window next to him. The sky was obscured by an overlapping mess of angry, purple-black thunderheads.

A loud explosion suddenly rocked the fuselage, followed by another in quick succession. Jefferey panicked immediately. He lurched forward and grabbed the intercom. "Captain, what the hell was that?" he demanded. There was no response. Another crash sounded even closer as the plane began to buck violently.

Several seats forward, Krishinko was yelling. "What the hell is going on?"

They were all wide awake now, looking out the windows and at each other in fear.

"Sorry for the bumpy ride folks. We've encountered some troublesome thunderheads. Please keep your seatbelts on. We've been trying to get around them, but the windows are pretty tight. There could be more rapid changes in altitude if we fly into rising or falling columns of air. Secure any loose items you might have so that they don't fly around the cabin. Thank you for your patience."

The cabin returned to silence until the next lightning bolt hit, perilously nearby.

Snow gripped the armrests of her seat and fought the panic she felt taking hold. She had many hours of flight time in military aircraft and had been through some very dicey moments, but she'd never flown through a thunderstorm. She knew the only reason they were attempting this route was because Typhon was out of time, and perhaps because they didn't have enough fuel to get around the front.

No sooner had she completed that thought when she was thrust upwards with great force. He seatbelt cut into her hips but held.

Loose items around the cabin were now pinned to the ceiling. It was impossible to tell if the plane was even still upright. The lights flickered out and the roar of the calamity inside and out all but drowned out the blaring emergency alarms. As the emergency lights dimly illuminated the aisleway and brilliant flashes lit up the windows. They dropped out of the clouds, and she could now see the horizon outside, only something was off. The far edge of the Earth was a straight vertical line, right through the middle of her window. The thunderclouds were there, but not above. Instead, they were along the right side, scrolling from bottom to top. Confused at first, she suddenly made sense of it. They were in a nosedive, corkscrewing downward to the sea.

CHAPTER THIRTY

QUESTIONS WITHOUT ANSWERS

Two hours later, their gear was packed and they were ready to move out. Mac's mobile again buzzed as the two men were slumped in their chairs. A half-eaten pizza and two empty Guinness bottles decorated the coffee table. Mac was already half awake, originally intent on keeping one eye on the receiver screen. At some point, he'd dozed off. He grabbed his phone as Franklin sat up, wiping his eyes.

"Sisco," Mac answered, putting the phone on speaker again.

"Mac," Clausen responded, "we have a general idea where they're going."

Mac's eyes darted to the screen. Franklin was already staring at it with a confused look. Clausen continued. "Their vector never changed. As long as they don't make a last-minute turn, they are either headed for Australia or New Zealand. That's the good news."

"Uh, Mac stuttered. "What's the bad news? I'm not seeing Snow's tracker anymore."

Clausen replied gravely. "Well, that's not good then."

"What do you mean?" Franklin jumped in as he stared worriedly at the screen. "What's the bad news?"

"They never filed a flight plan. Their transponder has been turned off and they haven't made any radio calls. And they've been out of radar contact. We picked them up briefly on satellite and were tracking them until they entered a very big line of thunderstorms. We never saw them come out the other side. If you've lost the signal on Snow's tracker, I think they could have gone down," Clausen answered softly.

"OK…" Franklin responded thoughtfully. "So, what do we do now… If they did go down, it'll probably take a while to know for sure. Hopefully the black box wasn't disabled. If they did, Typhon's leadership is decapitated. That's a good thing. Too bad about Snow, unless she was one of them. If so, good riddance."

Mac shook his head.

"We won't be certain about anything until we can do some digging. We are already checking with the countries nearest to their last known position. It will take some time to get search and rescue resources out there due to the distance and the weather."

"What do you want us to do, Admiral?" Mac asked.

"Come on home, join your team, and we'll get to the bottom of this together," Clausen answered.

It was a somber flight for Mac and Franklin as they reflected on the events of the past few days. Franklin was able to catch up on badly needed sleep, but Mac was too worked up. He was still trying to figure things out. In his view, there were only three things that would account for the lost signal. Either someone discovered the tracker and destroyed it, Jasmine destroyed it, or the aircraft had, in fact, crashed into the ocean. It could have malfunctioned, perhaps, if the plane was hit by lightning. But Mac dismissed that as unlikely. The receiver case lay open on his lap. Mac had been staring at the screen for three hours now with the hope Jasmin's little dot would suddenly reappear. He chuckled then, wondering how pissed off Martin was going to be when he realized they stole it. It was OK though; Clausen would bail him out. And hopefully, he would have more insight for Mac by the time they landed in Maryland.

It was early afternoon by the time Mac and Franklin checked into NSA headquarters and made their way through security to the ninth floor. Admiral Clausen was waiting in the lobby of his executive suite and greeted them warmly.

"Good afternoon gentlemen, I hope you had a good flight and were able to get a little shut eye."

"The flight was fine Admiral, the sleep, not so much," Mac answered.

"We still have a lot of questions without answers," Clausen said as he ushered them into the conference room.

"Is the rest of the team joining?" Mac asked.

"They're all inside."

Clausen opened the door, and they went in. Swan was closest and group hugged Mac and Franklin.

Curry slapped them both on the back. "Good to see you home safe!"

Peter Singe, seated at the table, smiled and yelled "welcome back guys! I thought I was going to have to fly over there to bail you out."

"I dare say gentlemen," Warsaw piped in, "you had us worried for a bit! Good to see you safe."

Mac held up his hands and said, "thanks guys, it's great to see you too and we're glad to be back where the smart people are, so we can get some answers."

Everyone in the room laughed lightheartedly.

"Alright team, let's take our seats and I will bring you up to speed," the Admiral directed. "First, thank you again, each of you, for your exemplary work throughout this mission. You have exceeded my expectations, and the President send his thanks. A lot has happened since our last full team briefing.

"The New York and Cayman Islands operations yielded invaluable and actionable intelligence. Curry and Swan," he pointed to each of them, "you uncovered damning details of Typhon's criminal financial activities and key details about the organization and its structure. Warsaw and Singe convinced two of Typhon's primary bankers to disclose critical financial commitments that Typhon was using to fund numerous operations around the world. Mac and Franklin engaged directly with Typhon operatives in London and Paris. Franklin took a hit for the team, but it was worth it. The information they gleaned was leading us directly to both Gundersons, Krishinko, and Von Stemp. Perhaps others. But they may have all perished along with the turncoat Jasmine Snow in the South China Sea—more to follow on that. Finally, they also discovered new information about a Typhon operation called *Chaos*. More to follow on that as well." He paused to sip his coffee.

"Admiral," Swan asked, "what progress have we made with all this raw intelligence? What is the analysis?"

"Quite a bit," Clausen nodded. "We've identified what we believe are a majority of their ongoing operations and building lists of individuals we think are involved. It's a big list. We have also been successful in decrypting much of their encrypted data. This will speed our progress. We are releasing some information, as we can, to NATCOG and the President is working with those countries' leaders. That's a slower, but crucial endeavor that will ultimately ensure we can dismantle Typhon across the globe."

"What about Chaos? What is it?" asked Curry.

"Too early to tell," answered the Admiral, "but what is implied by its name doesn't seem good. It could be a Plan B they have in place that will mitigate our current efforts against them."

"Which brings us to the $64,000 question," Mac added. "You said 'more to follow.' Do we know anything else about Typhon's aircraft and the status of those aboard?"

Everyone looked at Clausen in anticipation.

He cleared his throat. "An international search and rescue mission has been initiated, but the weather has been brutal at those coordinates for a couple days, so progress will be slow."

"What about the black box?" asked Singe.

"The SAR team has not told us they've received a ping, as of yet." Clausen replied.

CHAPTER THIRTY-ONE

WRAPPING UP

The team stayed busy for the next few days with debriefings and meetings to go over new intel as it trickled in. Clausen continued his mole hunt and held daily conversations with President Holbrook. Three days after Mac and Franklin returned from France, the Admiral called the entire team to the ninth floor to discuss the future of Team Apogee.

Once they were seated, the Admiral began. "I know you have been anticipating this day with mixed feelings, and I feel the same. Despite our collective misgivings, it is time to wrap up field operations. Our plan from the outset was to identify the Typhon leadership and main operators, share our intelligence, and allow NATCOG member countries to deploy their own intelligence and law enforcement agencies to take appropriate action while we do the same here in the U.S. The first part of that, the part Apogee played, is complete. The rest is ongoing."

"You are to be congratulated and should be very proud of what you've accomplished. Without your efforts, the world as we know it would have continued to spiral downward. We're not even sure at this point what the end state would have looked like. Few people will ever know of your accomplishments, but as you know we're not in this business for the recognition."

"Sir," Mac interjected, should we assume there is no news on the aircraft?"

"Search and rescue has expanded the search area, but unless they find something soon, they will suspend operations by the end of the week. At that point we can safely assume all on board perished."

Mac nodded. "I understand. And forgive me if I'm out of place here, but I'd like to request you keep us operational until the end of the search. I have a bad feeling things aren't exactly what they appear. And even if I'm wrong, we can help here with analysis."

Clausen sat back in his chair. "You know, when I tell you something like this, I've already run it by the President, and he's already agreed. So, I can't do what you're asking, not formally, anyway. But you can stick around for the rest of the week. If something changes, I can recommend to the President that Apogee be reinstated, and we'll have a head start."

"Fair enough," Mac replied. It was semantics, really. He got what he wanted.

The search officially ended two days later, however. And as planned, so did Team Apogee. They got together at Mac's house for drinks, then headed to Cantler's for a crab dinner. As the night wore down, Franklin proposed a toast. All eyes turned towards him.

He raised his mug. "To life, liberty, and the pursuit of happiness."

"Here, here!" the group yelled in unison.

Mac bade them all good night and went home. It was a nice evening and the fitting end to a difficult mission. He was exhausted and wasted no time hitting the sack, his eyes closing almost as soon as his head hit the pillow.

And then he was back on the rock. He was leading someone up a steep cliff face. As he grabbed a nub of granite barely big enough to hold on to, he heard a faint a faint buzzing noise from somewhere nearby. A bee? He ignored it. This move was too risky to screw up. He had to focus. He didn't want to fall. There it was again, and it was getting closer. He let go of the nub and swatted near his ear. His right foot began to slip, and he reached for the nub again, but too late. He began to fall.

Mac suddenly woke from his dream. His mobile was skittering across the nightstand towards him, its display glaring obnoxiously. Mac grabbed it. A text from 'Unknown.' It was 3:30 am. He unlocked his phone and tapped the message app. Just four words, and they sent a jolt of adrenaline coursing through his veins:

We are alive—Jasmine.

♦

To be continued in THE TYPHON AFFAIR

AFTERWORD

I wrote this book and its sequel, *The Typhon Affair*, at the height of the Covid-19 Pandemic. Even though this work was intended to be contemporary, I elected not to weave Covid in. To do so could marginalize the seriousness of the global politico-cultural devolution that is central to the plots of both books.

While the primary objective of *Apogee* is to entertain, I cannot deny my interest in making a salient point. It appears to many that the current state of humanity is in decline. We are rapidly losing the ability to effectively govern ourselves. While there is much to be said for new ways of doing things and adopting change with the goal of improvement, it is equally important to consult history, and to recognize that what is best for the minority is not always best for the majority. There must be balance. Diminished vocabularies, ignorance of and rewriting history, demonizing faiths, eradicating personal freedoms in favor of federal control, intolerance of the individualism and the freedoms that are the bedrock of a Democratic Republic form of government—the list goes on. The term for this is 'cancel culture' and it is an existential threat to our nation and the world.

Apogee is just a story that tells of a world situation not unlike what is happening now. The societal disruptions described in Apogee are happening today. That is not fiction. The idea that a conspiracy could be at work might seem like fiction, but don't be so quick to dispel the possibility.

Down the rabbit hole, we begin to see patterns: organization, funding and incentivization. Centralized government control. Censorship, misleading and outright untrue journalism. But is there someone at the top pulling all the strings? Money begets power begets control. It is an unrelenting, vicious circle that only gets tighter and stronger, and it is man's greatest sin. Apogee may be no more than another tall tale for many, but I do hope it will shine a light on the state of our human condition and cause some to ask, *who is pulling the strings?*

—*Lou Earle*

ABOUT THE AUTHOR

Lou Earle is a writer, entrepreneur, and business executive with roots in corporate America. He graduated from the University of Pennsylvania and served four years in the United States Navy as a member of the Naval Security Group during the Vietnam War. He spent his final two years of service at the National Security Agency (NSA) in Fort Meade, Maryland.

Lou was the founding Chairman of Badgerdog Literary Publishing Company, a not-for-profit that published the literary digest *American Short Fiction* and provided outreach writing courses through Youth Voices in Ink for disenfranchised children in central Texas. He is also the owner, CEO, and publisher of *Austin Fit Magazine*, a health and fitness publication.

Lou is married with three children and three grandchildren. He and his wife Lynne live on a ranch in Wimberley, Texas with a menagerie of furry friends including two horses, one mammoth donkey, two miniature bulls, five dogs and five chickens.